"Stop! You've

She pulled bac[k]
trying to resist[,]
him.

His expression changed to one of
incredulity. "Why? What did I do,
Laurel? What's wrong?"

"Just *stop!*"

He frowned, his look intense and
penetrating. "Are you trying to
tell me that you don't *want* me?"

"You must know I do. But, Evan . . .
I—"

"You *what*, Laurel?"

"Evan, this can't happen. Please, you
have to understand!" She paused, her
mind racing. "Evan, I've never . . ."

A small, unpleasant half smile formed
on his lips. "Oh? You've *never?* I
wonder why I don't believe that."

CARIN SCOFIELD
traces her love of writing to her grandmother,
and her love of travel and the American landscape to her explorer/ancestor Kit Carson. An
avowed romantic, she loves fog, candlelight,
roaring fires and writing books that reflect the
beauties and possibilities of love.

Dear Reader:

Silhouette Books is pleased to announce the creation of a new line of contemporary romances—*Silhouette Special Editions*. Each month we'll bring you six new love stories written by the best of today's authors—Janet Dailey, Brooke Hastings, Laura Hardy, Sondra Stanford, Linda Shaw, Patti Beckman, and many others.

Silhouette Special Editions are written with American women in mind; they are for readers who want more: more story, more details and descriptions, more realism, and more *romance*. *Special Editions* are longer than most contemporary romances allowing for a closer look at the relationship between hero and heroine with emphasis on heightened romantic tension and greater sensuous and sensual detail. If you want more from a romance, be sure to look for *Silhouette Special Editions* on sale this February wherever you buy books.

We welcome any suggestions or comments, and I invite you to write us at the address below.

Karen Solem
Editor-in-Chief
Silhouette Books
P.O. Box 769
New York, N. Y. 10019

CARIN SCOFIELD
Winterfire

Silhouette *Romance*

Published by Silhouette Books New York

America's Publisher of Contemporary Romance

SILHOUETTE BOOKS, a Simon & Schuster Division of
GULF & WESTERN CORPORATION
1230 Avenue of the Americas, New York, N.Y. 10020

ISBN: 0-671-57122-2

First Silhouette Books printing December, 1981

10 9 8 7 6 5 4 3 2 1

America's Publisher of Contemporary Romance

Printed in the U.S.A.

Winterfire

Chapter One

Laurel Martin stepped off the plane into the last light of a wan winter sunset and air so crisp and chill that it startled her to breathe it. She had known she was going to a part of the country where February meant ice and snow and cold, but suddenly emerging into it was a shock. Invigorating, bracing—but a shock all the same.

Later, in the car, she noticed that dusk came quickly here. Night had gathered within a few short minutes. Nothing was visible outside now but the black-and-white world of smooth, dark road and snowy roadside fences and the tracery of trees that loomed up in the headlights and disappeared behind them. Cameron, the portly and deferential butler-chauffeur-factotum from the castle who had met her flight, was at ease at the wheel. "The road's been cleared all the way, Miss Martin," he told her. "The snow crews do a fine job."

7

He glanced at his watch. "We should be at Winterfire in about half an hour."

"I'm anxious to see it," Laurel said.

Winterfire. The Templar family castle. This was Laurel's first important solo assignment as assistant curator of the museum's Antiquities Department, and she had made the trip with mixed feelings.

On the one hand, she was delighted about it. The assignment was an honor—usually such a mission was entrusted to an older, more experienced member of the staff. The directors and Dr. Spence had shown great trust in her by choosing her to handle it, and she appreciated the vote of confidence, though she knew she was perfectly capable of doing the job.

On the other hand, Richard Bellamy, her fiancé, had kept harping on the great responsibility they were asking her to undertake—until after a while she had grown a bit apprehensive. The Templar acquisition *was* priceless. It *would* be up to her to accept it for the museum and deliver it back there intact and undamaged. Richard had begged her not to go, bringing up his objections over and over—even their parting early that morning at San Diego International Airport had been strained—until finally she had absorbed some of his negativism. When she thought about it, she was rather hurt by his lack of trust in her. Oh well. She shrugged her doubts away and turned her thoughts to the Templar Papers, the reason for the trip.

The Templar Papers were a set of parchment pages illuminated with intricate lettering and artwork that had been executed centuries ago in Europe, one of only two such sets in the world. The other set was still in France, privately owned by an aristocratic family and not accessible to the public. The Templar collection had been owned by the American branch of the same noble family for more than two hundred years, and now the owner, Miss Dana Templar, had passed on. In her will she had bequeathed the Templar Papers to the museum because of her longtime friendship with Dr. Spence, curator of the Antiquities Department and Laurel's boss.

Dr. Spence had been overjoyed at the news of the bequest, but terribly upset. He could not leave the museum to personally bring back the papers—not for months. Too many urgent matters demanded his presence at the museum. So he and the directors had deputized Laurel to go.

She thought of the things Dr. Spence had told her about Winterfire Castle, the Templar family home. She had listed intently, if a bit indulgently, privately thinking that Dr. Spence's fondness for Miss Dana and his pleasant memories of Winterfire had surely colored his descriptions of the castle and its treasures, at least to some extent. Such a fantasylike place as he described could hardly exist!

Cameron slowed the car and brought a small remote-control unit out of his coat pocket. He touched a button on it as they approached the entrance to a private, wooded lane. As they turned into it Laurel saw the great iron gates that stood there—gates blazoned with a heavy metal rose entwined with the letter *T*—open and swing inward. The modern equivalent of a moat and drawbridge, Laurel thought; perhaps Dr. Spence hadn't exaggerated after all!

They drove through the gateway and into the lane; the gates closed automatically behind them. At last they rounded a sweeping curve and emerged from the evergreen overhang that canopied the road, and Winterfire Castle lay before them.

Lit by flaming torches in a pristine setting of snow, the castle glimmered. Drawing closer, Laurel saw that the torches were set atop long lancelike poles set beside the massive entrance. It *was* the way Dr. Spence had said it would be. If anything, he had underplayed it. It was spellbinding, it was enchanting—something from a fairy tale, a thing captured at the height of its glory in the Middle Ages and preserved untouched. All it needs, Laurel thought, is a pair of wolfhounds— and liveried pages with trumpets to open the door!

As Cameron drew up before the torchlit entrance Laurel reminded herself that it was, after all, a miniaturized replica of the Templar family's European stronghold, and that it was modern in every way—it only *looked* like a medieval castle. It stood in upper New York State, and this was the twentieth century, and for all its charm, it was not really unique. But it *was* stunning.

In the entrance hall, Laurel's attention was immediately drawn by the portrait. It would have been impossible not to notice it; from its position above the landing of the great curved ebony and gilt staircase, it dominated everything below. It was magnificent. The antique frame hung from heavy bronze chains, and the subject seemed to say, "I am in charge here, make no mistake about that!" His eyes glinted arrogantly straight down into Laurel's, surveying her with serene superiority. She felt the impact of that look with an almost physical reaction. Something about the portrait—its vivid lifelike quality, the sheer overpowering maleness of the man—reached out and down and into her. The feeling was confusing. It was almost as though she stood unclothed, vulnerable and helpless, before a living man. Then, laughing at herself, she tossed her head, her red-gold hair flaring. "Who is he?" she asked.

Cameron started to reply, but just then two women came into the room, and their greetings and Cameron's introductions drove the question from her mind. It was not until later, at dinner, seated across from Denise Jordan, the young woman who had been Miss Dana Templar's secretary, that Laurel learned about the man in the portrait.

"That's Evan Templar," Denise informed Laurel. "He was the last master of Winterfire. He . . . died last fall."

"Oh?" Laurel was surprised. Something had been left out of Dr. Spence's briefings. He had not mentioned a "master" of Winterfire—only the long-ago Templars and Miss Dana. "I hadn't known."

Denise's friendly young face was serious. "Miss Dana brought Evan up after his parents died. He was like the son she never had. Then, when he had grown up, he had some kind of awful experience—I never found out what it was. Miss Dana never liked to talk about anything that had hurt him, so I didn't ask too many questions. Anyway, he went away."

"He . . . went away?"

"Into the Foreign Legion."

"The Foreign Legion?" Laurel exclaimed. "Good grief, I didn't know it even existed anymore!"

"Oh, it does. And Evan served in it. Just as some of the other Templar men did before him. I know that from the records in the archives." Denise paused. "He'd been away almost five years—they join for a five-year enlistment, you know—so it was almost time for him to return home. But then, last November, Miss Dana got the cable. He'd been listed first as missing, and then as killed in action." Denise's eyes were sad. "She passed away soon after. And now Winterfire is in probate, along with the rest of the estate—all of the family's business holdings and property. I suppose Winterfire will be sold. There are already several prospective buyers who've expressed an interest. Mr. Cain is handling all the legalities. You're acquainted with him, aren't you?"

"Yes. He contracted Dr. Spence about the papers. And I've talked with him on the phone. We're supposed to meet here tomorrow evening about the bequest."

Denise nodded. "Yes, he told me." Then she said, "He and I are working together. That is, since I was Miss Dana's secretary, he thought it would be sensible for me to do the inventory of her personal effects and writings, update the lists of things that have accumulated in the archives, double-check the catalogue of artworks in the castle, that sort of thing."

"I see." Laurel pondered the things Denise had told her as she sipped the dark aromatic coffee Cameron had brought to go with dessert, and the conversation soon turned to other topics.

Later, as Denise was getting ready to leave, she said, "I can stay over if you'd like me to, Laurel."

"That's not necessary, but thanks."

"Well, I just thought—you'll be the only one in the castle. Cameron and Bridget live in what used to be the carriage house, and Toddy—he's the groom—lives up over the stables. But there won't be anybody *inside* but you. So if you'd be more comfortable, it's no problem for me to—"

"I'll be fine, really!" Laurel assured her, laughing. "I'm just going to make a few notes in my work journal, call Dr. Spence, and sleep. I'm pretty tired."

"Then I'll run along." Denise buttoned her coat. "See you in the morning."

On the way up to her bedroom, Laurel paused on the landing to examine the portrait more closely. The last Evan Templar had been incredibly attractive in a dark and rough-hewn way. The curious combination of masterful disdain and boyishness fascinated Laurel. She had a deep appreciation for well-executed works of art, but no portrait that she could remember had ever intrigued her so strongly before. The man in this painting had obviously had enormous magnetism, and the artist had caught it unerringly. There was a power that lay in the eyes and reached out and *dared* one to look away.

The face was rugged, with a straight Roman nose, an unsmiling but generous mouth, and a cleft chin. Something caught her eye and she peered closely at it: a tiny scar that marred the otherwise smooth skin of the face just under one temple. What had done that? It was oddly shaped. The point of a sword could have caused it, she thought.

So this had been Evan Templar VI, last of the ancestral line. He'd been clean-shaven, and his thick, unruly thatch of black hair lay above his high forehead with one stray lock falling forward.

The picture had been painted seven years ago, she thought, reading the date beneath the artist's signature. He had been about twenty-five then, probably. Yes, he was indeed the master of Winterfire, she thought. That's plain to see! Look at the set of that head, the pride in that face!

The downstairs clock began to chime eleven. She turned away from the portrait and continued up the handsome staircase to her bedroom.

Laurel had showered. She wore a flowing peach-colored chiffon gown that billowed behind her as she crossed the room barefoot to the ancient canopy bed. Someone—Bridget?—had turned back the satin quilted coverlet to reveal smooth ivory sheets and pillows with a heavily embroidered rose entwined with a *T* on their cases. The bed things were deliciously perfumed with the scent of roses.

As she turned she glimpsed the scene beyond her window and went to stand at the casement and look out. Awash with silver moonlight, snow lay thick upon the hills below, rounding them into soft shadow shapes, and dark bushy evergreen groves smudged the landscape. Solid dark shadows indicated the carriage house and the stables. The moon, a thin wafer of pale lemon, hung impaled upon the slender shaft of a solitary pine. Everything below seemed luminous, glowing dreamlike in the cold moonlight.

The insistent jangle of the telephone dragged Laurel up from her deep sleep, jolting her awake. She groped for the light switch, turned on the bedside lamp, and lifted the receiver. The clock downstairs chimed two as she said sleepily, "Hello?"

Richard's wide-awake voice said, "Hello, Laurel! Laurel? Hello!"

She came slowly awake. Richard said, "Forgive me, darling! I'd dialed the number and it had rung several times before I realized there's a three-hour time difference between here and there. I know I woke you. I'm sorry."

"It's all right, Richard."

"I called to make sure you were all right. Why didn't you call me?"

"I was going to in the morning." Laurel sat up, shook the coppery tangle of her hair back from her shoulders, and added, "I called Dr. Spence and told him I'd arrived and everything was all right. Didn't he call you?"

"Well, yes. But I wanted to hear it from *you*." Richard paused. Laurel read his mood. He was being mildly reproving, letting her know without words that he was disappointed in her for not calling him immediately upon her arrival. She frowned slightly. *Why* was he being this way? she wondered. He went on. "I was worried about the last part of the trip—that commuter airline. Those little planes . . ."

"The trip was fine; I'm fine; *everything* is fine, Richard—and, oh," she said, her voice warming, "you should see Winterfire! Everywhere I look I see something unique and beautiful—"

"I don't really want to hear about the place, Laurel," he cut in. His tone surprised her. Now he sounded almost rude. "I'm not calling long distance at eleven o'clock at night—"

"Two o'clock in the morning, Richard—"

"—to hear about some *castle*. I called to make sure my fiancée is all right. I'm concerned about you." Then, more softly, he added, "I love you. Don't you know that?" Now he sounded rueful, as though by making the trip she had wronged him in some way. What had gotten into him? she wondered, irritated. This trip was business—why couldn't he understand that?

At that moment there was a sound on the line—a

sound that shouldn't have been there. It was a small, muffled sound, almost like a chuckle. Laurel heard it clearly. "Richard, are you on an extension phone?"

"No, why do you ask?" Richard apparently hadn't heard anything.

"Nothing. No reason." But she *had* heard something, she hadn't imagined it—and Richard hadn't made that sound.

They talked for a few more moments, and at last Richard sounded more like himself, mollified and placated by her assurances that she missed him, that she would call him often, and that she would return to San Diego in a very short time. She wished, as she said those things, that he hadn't made her feel so defensive, almost apologetic about the trip. His attitude disturbed her. He'd always been gentle and loving and unselfish —until the New York trip had come up. Then something had seemed to change. He had become . . . possessive. Jealous. Of her *work*.

Thinking that, she felt disloyal. She reminded herself that his attitude only reflected his love; it was just that the way he expressed it was irritating.

Finally they said good night and Richard hung up. Laurel was just about to replace the receiver at her end, had in fact taken it away from her ear and extended her arm to hang it up, when she heard another sound that shouldn't have been there. It was the unmistakable sound of another phone being replaced on its cradle— and it was not thousands of miles away in California, it was right *here!* Here, on this telephone line!

Alarmed, eyes wide, Laurel dropped the receiver and stared at it. And then the thought came: Of course, Bridget and Cameron must have an extension in the carriage house, or there was one in the stables, and somebody had lifted the phone to see if the call was for them. What could be more natural?

Relieved, she turned off the lamp and snuggled down into the warm nest of her bed again to sleep.

Laurel was looking for Denise. She'd been working in the library earlier, but she'd gone off somewhere while Laurel had been upstairs. Laurel looked into the den, found it deserted, and went on to the library.

The room's dimness surprised her; the drapes had been drawn against the glaring outside light and no lamps had been turned on. A fire leaped in the stone fireplace, sending dancing lights about the room. Laurel closed the door and glanced about. The room was lined with shelves housing thousands of books. In the center stood a heavy refectory table strewn with Denise's lists of documents. A sofa faced the fireplace, its back to the room.

Laurel hesitated, wondering whether to wait for Denise here or elsewhere. Laurel was eager to see the famous Templar Papers at last, and Denise had promised to show them to her. Where had she gone? Laurel wondered, crossing to a shelf of contemporary novels. She decided she would select one and read to pass the time until Denise appeared. Slowly her eyes adjusted to the dusky gloom.

As she stepped around the table she was conscious of a movement, a shadow, really, beyond the back of the sofa. She looked—and halted, staring. For there, rising lazily to face her, was *Evan Templar!* The same unsmiling, haughty, slightly mocking face she had studied in the portrait now turned to meet her shocked gaze. He was alive, and he was here!

His expression did not change. He came around the

sofa slowly, moving with the grace—and menace—of a panther. Laurel stood thunderstruck, trying to grasp what she was seeing.

He reached out his hand to her and said, "So we meet at last. It's a pleasure, Miss Martin. Welcome to Winterfire."

Laurel's face had gone white and she said nothing. He raised her hand to his lips, palm upward, and brushed it with a kiss. She drew her hand away as though in slow motion. Her mind floundered, racing between *he can't be here, this can't be happening,* and the undeniable fact that he *was* there, living, breathing, and as sardonically autocratic as his portrait had foretold.

He towered over her. He still did not smile; in fact, he seemed angry. His eyes moved slowly over her hair, her face, her parted lips, then downward, as though he had every right, to the soft mounds of her breasts beneath the low-cut emerald jersey dress that she wore. There his gaze lingered until at last she moved, uncomfortable beneath his scrutiny. He completed his proprietary inspection slowly, deliberately, and finally he nodded as though in amused approval. Laurel, recovering, beginning to feel irritated at his manner, said, "I . . . was told . . . that you were . . ." Her voice trailed off in embarrassment.

"Dead?" He laughed, but it was a chill, mirthless laugh. The intense power of the man reached out from his blue-green eyes, lashing like a stormy sea. "Miss Martin, as somebody once said when he read his own obituary in the newspaper—wasn't it Mark Twain?— 'the reports of my death have been greatly exaggerated.' No, I am not deceased, as you can see."

"The cable—"

"The cable to my aunt was a mistake. I was separated from my unit and it took me a while to get back, that's all." He paused, a cloud lowering darkly in his eyes. "It's hard to take the fact that she died without knowing. But there was no way I could have changed that—I didn't even know they'd sent her a message reporting me missing, let alone killed in action! I knew nothing of that, or of her death, until I returned to the States." He spoke as though to himself; his eyes were remote. "I hadn't expected anything to be changed. I don't know what I expected—certainly not what I found! My aunt gone, everybody under the impression that *I* was dead too, lawyers busily analyzing wills, people making lists and getting ready to sell my home! Vultures circling, getting ready to swoop down and sack the place—" He broke off, a study in subdued fury. The muscles of his face flexed as he clenched his teeth.

Laurel gasped, her mind reeling. His words stung her like a slap, a physical assault. She took a step backward. *Vultures!*

What a cruel, ugly thing to say—and *he meant her!* she thought, stunned. Anger kindled within her and she found her voice. "Mr. Templar," she said, lifting her chin, her eyes shooting sparks of newborn fury, "I'm glad you've returned, alive and well. And I'm sorry about your aunt and all the rest. But your aunt's attorney, Mr. Cain, can explain to you the reason why I came. I assure you I've no intention of—of being a *vulture.*" Her voice had become husky with emotion. "I'll leave immediately." She turned to go.

He caught her arm. "Why on earth—? You just got here!" And he smiled, and Laurel was caught entirely off guard. "Don't you like it here?"

She stared at him. *"Like* it here? What's that got to do with anything? Of course I like it here. It's beautiful. I meant—"

He waved his hand, dismissing what she was saying. "I know what you meant. I know all about it. I talked with Mr. Cain yesterday evening, when I first got back." He looked Laurel up and down again, this time with smoldering appreciation. "I asked him to keep my arrival from you; I wanted to introduce myself. But let's discuss all that later, shall we?"

Confused, Laurel hesitated. Her thoughts were whirling. Of course he had been shocked to arrive back home after five years to find things in a state of upheaval, and furious to find *her* here, ready to take away a priceless heirloom. That was understandable. But then—why didn't he want her to leave at once?

A sudden ray of hope shone in her mind. He had loved his aunt dearly; she had willed the papers to the museum, even though she had no right to do so. But she had *thought* she had, of course, because she made that will thinking she was the sole surviving Templar. Was it possible he would honor his aunt's wishes and let the museum have the papers?

Not very likely, she thought. After he had said what he did, after he had called her a vulture?

But he hadn't actually said he would *not* give the papers to the museum! Not in so many words, anyway.

Evan's mood had softened. "I must say, you reacted better to seeing me than Bridget did. She fainted! And when she came to, it took me a while to calm her down. I sent her off to bed to rest up. Cameron's looking after her. You didn't faint, you just froze." He took her hand again and led her around the sofa. They sat down, facing the flames. "I suppose I should have had Mr.

Cain announce me instead of just appearing and scaring people out of their wits. But I was busy with my own problems, and I always prefer to handle things myself."

He didn't look at her; he gazed into the flames instead. Firelight played on his sculptured face, lighting it with little flashes of gold. Inexplicably, she was disappointed that they had met in these circumstances. What was he like, she wondered, with his friends? With his women? Surely any man who looked like he did had no lack of women. . . .

For some reason the thought bothered her, and she hastened to remind herself that she was an engaged woman.

She sat there watching him, unsure of what to say, how to proceed. She felt fairly certain that if she asked him outright at this point whether or not the museum would get the papers in accordance with Miss Dana's will, he would explode and say no.

The professional, competent part of her mind that had been trained to handle difficult situations in her work warned: *Caution. Handle this right and maybe, just maybe, the museum will still get the papers. Wait and see. There is the chance that he'll decide to be generous. Maybe you won't have to go back to San Diego empty-handed.*

So she remained beside him. He had slipped into a reverie, totally unaware of her presence, his face expressionless. His thigh, in tight-fitting navy pants, did not quite touch hers, but she felt his nearness physically, like the heat from the open fire before them. The lines of him, the rugged profile of his face, his rock-hard chin with its little cleft, the tiny scar at his temple, the muscles of his shoulders under the V-necked velour shirt, held her there beside him, fascinated, immobile.

The skin of his exposed chest was tan, his muscles hard and lean. She saw the rise and fall of his chest as he breathed. She had an almost unbearable impulse to touch that tan skin, to tangle her fingers in the dark, wiry curls that nestled there. The artist had painted him faithfully, she thought; he had caught the banked fires inside him, and the passion. . . .

Suddenly rousing from his silence, Evan turned to face Laurel. "Forgive me. I'm not being a very good host." The flickering red flames were reflected in his eyes as he scanned her face. "I almost forgot; there's a family tradition."

And before she was aware of what was happening, Evan had taken her hands, stood up, and drawn her to stand before him, then pulled her gently into his arms. He held her captive there, pinioned helplessly against him, her pulses fluttering like a butterfly's wings. He looked deep into her eyes, then lowered his mouth to hers, claiming her parted lips, kissing her softly and then with growing hardness, his heartbeat thundering against her breast, the steel-hard muscles of his body pressing against her. Astonishment, quick fury, and outrage crashed through Laurel's consciousness, and she tried to beat her fists against him. Then, madly, without her volition, her senses soared on the growing wave of sweet desire that his lips ignited within her, and she answered his kiss, letting the flow of this new ecstasy build as the kiss went on and on. Finally, when he was quite ready, he drew gently away and released her. Standing, his arms at his sides, he looked somberly down into her eyes. "There," he said. "Now you've been officially welcomed to Winterfire."

"What do you mean? How dare you . . . ?"

"I told you, it's a family tradition. Don't blame me; I

didn't invent it!" He was mocking her, looking at her with a maddening little-boy grin. "The tradition of welcoming women to Winterfire—not all of them, just some—goes way back. Clear back to the very first twig on the family tree, maybe. I don't know."

"I don't believe you!"

"It's true. There's an old poem about it somewhere in the archives. Let's see if I can remember it. *'Kiss the one who has the power/To change your life within an hour,/But touch you not the fireless one,/Lest all your hopes be sad undone.'"*

Laurel said nothing. Her heart was racing. She was shaking with anger. But the poem *was* lovely—if she could believe he hadn't made it up on the spot! Needlessly, she straightened her dress, then took a long, shuddering breath. Evan watched her, amusement dancing in his eyes. She turned her back to him, unconsciously touching her lips; the tingling, almost bruised sensation lingered, along with the memory of his rock-hard body, the intensity of him, the power, the pinewoods and sea-foam way his skin smelled—and her anger began to subside, to be replaced with a wave of guilt. She was *engaged.* She reminded herself again of that fact as forcefully as she could, glancing at her third finger, left hand, on which sparkled Richard Bellamy's ring.

The guilt that she felt was dispelled, almost, by the common-sense realization that what had happened had not been her doing. She had certainly not brought it about. It had all been his fault—the master of Winterfire had taken advantage. Yet there lingered a tiny shred of disapproval within her conscience that said: *But you liked it. You didn't really mind it at all.*

She went to the cloister table in the middle of the

room and drummed her fingertips on it, ordering her
emotions to halt their tumult. She felt his eyes on her
back, and the sensation unnerved her almost as much
as his kiss had done.

She had to say something. Anything, she thought, to
break this silence, to make him stop watching her. She
decided to ask him if she could just *see* the papers.
Surely he couldn't object to that.

She turned to ask the question just as the library
door quietly closed. He was gone, and Laurel felt
strangely bereft.

Frowning at her own discomfiture, Laurel tried to
shake the mood away. She crossed the room to fling
open the drapes, letting the golden light in. It flooded
the room, glancing off polished figurines and bric-a-
brac, gleaming on old leather book bindings, lying in
butter-colored patches on the cream carpet.

She went to the reference books, selected the *F*
volume of an encyclopedia, and took it to the sofa. For
the next few minutes, Laurel occupied herself with
learning all that the book had to say about the French
Foreign Legion, or, as it was properly called, the
Légion Étrangère.

". . . Colorful, gallant unit of the French govern-
ment . . . made up of foreign volunteers, Frenchmen
cannot join . . . men of the *Légion* must be between 18
and 40 years of age, in superb physical condition . . .

"An air of mystery, glamor, heroism surrounds the
Légion . . . some join to escape punishment for a
crime, some for adventure, some for other, private
reasons . . .

"King Louis Philippe originated the *Légion* in 1831
. . . present headquarters are at Aubagne, France,
near Marseille . . .

"The *Légion* has served all over the world, valorously defending the defenseless . . . noble . . . romantic . . ."

Laurel closed the book and replaced it on the shelf. She had learned a little about the *Légion Étrangère*—but nothing at all about why the Templar men had traditionally given five years of their lives to its service.

Nor why this Evan Templar, master of Winterfire, had spent half a decade with the Foreign Legion—the Legion of Strangers.

Nor why it should matter in the slightest to her.

Chapter Two

Laurel had entered the fact of Evan Templar's return to Winterfire in her work journal, but she had not called Dr. Spence to tell him the electrifying news. She knew she should. She realized that he had to be informed at once; the museum had already sent out media releases and arranged for special showings of the papers. She had to tell Dr. Spence to hold off on doing anything further until she found out whether or not the museum would in fact receive the papers.

She knew beyond a doubt that if she called Dr. Spence at this point, he would order her back to California instantly and send someone else, or come himself, to deal with the situation. He would never give up the papers without a fight, and he would want a real heavyweight to do the fighting.

But, she rationalized, she *was* qualified. She had all

the credentials. She could handle the situation as well as anyone—because it was a certainty that if Evan Templar had decided not to let the museum have the papers, *nobody* was going to change his mind about it.

And so, as the afternoon shadows lengthened outside on the glistening snow and evening approached, Laurel tried to put the matter out of her mind for the moment. She would wait until she knew what Evan intended to do before she called Dr. Spence. A few hours wouldn't make much difference.

Laurel was dressing for the dinner meeting with Mr. Cain. Wearing wispy flesh-colored underthings, she glanced at her reflection. It wasn't a *bad* face, she thought, inspecting it objectively. Laurel considered herself somewhat between plain and fairly attractive when she thought about it at all; never did she think "beautiful" in connection with herself. Where she saw simply good skin, others noticed a creamy, glowing complexion like the finish of a Dresden figurine; others saw her "average" nose as a short, straight, perfect one; where she saw her features as regular, the impression others received was of fresh, appealing loveliness. Her rich, ripe-red mouth was enchanting when she smiled, her elusive dimples adding charm. Dark, thick lashes shaded her honey-amber eyes, eyes that had golden flecks, like little fires, shining somewhere deep within them. Her brows were straight little wings. Laurel could never decide about her hair—was it blond or red? Too long? Was there too much of it? Others saw cascades of golden-red hair that caught the light and bounced as she walked, its luxuriant length ending in ringlets below her shoulders.

Laurel considered her body all right, but others saw a lovely form with high, rounded, firm young breasts, a small waist, trim, curving hips, and shapely legs. Looking at her reflection now in the mirror, she thought that her body was not the figure of a high-fashion model, but it served the purpose.

She heard explosive sounds from outside, below. Thunder? *Hoofbeats?* She ran to the window and looked down, and for a moment saw nothing. Then a darker shadow in the growing shadows of dusk, a moving shape that dashed out of the evergreens from the direction of the stables, the silhouette of a man on horseback, came galloping toward the castle. Laurel saw the horse swerve, following the walkway, and then horse and rider disappeared around the north side of the castle and she could see them no more.

Evan Templar, of course, Laurel thought. And obviously angry about something, judging from the way he had been riding. . . .

Laurel had still not decided what to wear for the dinner meeting. It would be an important business conference, and she wanted to look her best. She drew out a gown she had selected for her honeymoon with Richard. It was a dress the color of flame, a dress she had almost not bought—a gown designed for a woman of great beauty. Its material was a soft, thin silk, gossamer-frail, and it clung to her figure, from the low square-cut neckline to the floor, as though molded to her body. It revealed by its very concealment every curve and hollow, shimmering with radiance as she walked. She held it in front of her, smoothed it, eyed her reflection speculatively, and decided no, not for this evening.

When she left the bedroom she wore a high-throated white knit dress with simple Grecian lines. It hung gracefully to the floor, its conservative cut showing nothing but her bare arms and shoulders; she had bought the dress for a tea at the museum, and she wore it now with the same feeling of correctness. She wore simple satin slippers with it and a plain gold chain.

Laurel had no idea of the stunning effect. When she left the bedroom and went slowly down the great staircase, she, not the portrait of the master of Winterfire, commanded all attention below; it was as though she dazzled the group in the entrance hall, for they gazed up at her as though beholding a vision.

And then she joined them, and the talk resumed. Denise introduced Mr. Cain; Cameron announced dinner; Bridget bustled about, ready to serve another of her wonderful meals.

Oddly, Evan Templar was not there.

The table gleamed with old silver and snowy linen, cut glass and hand-wrought lace. Above, an enormous chandelier cast facets of light over the room, and candles on the table shed a soft glow. In the center of the table a cluster of ruby-red roses in a silver bowl caught Laurel's eye.

"The Templar rose," said Mr. Cain.

"What?"

"The famous Templar rose. These are representative of them at their best," he said. "Right, Cameron?"

Cameron halted on his way to the kitchen and turned to answer. "Yes, indeed."

And Laurel remembered. The Templar rose *had* been included in Dr. Spence's briefings. Long, long ago, the legend went, a beautiful young girl—daughter of one of the ancient Templars, in France, at the family's original castle of which Winterfire was a replica —had fallen in love with a gallant young knight who was going away on one of the Crusades. They planned to be married when he returned. In the castle garden there grew a particular rose of such beauty and glowing ruby-red color that it was the envy of all other nearby rose fanciers, and it had the added unique quality of living on almost indefinitely when cut. This rose had become the symbol of anything lasting, and changeless, and true. And so, when the young knight made ready to leave, he had cut a perfectly formed rose from the vine and given it to her, saying, "Take this rose and keep it in memory of its source. And it will live, until I see you again." And the rose did live . . . but he never returned, and the girl never married; she spent her life alone. It was she who designed the Templar coat of arms—a single red rose on a field of snow.

"It's a beautiful story," Laurel said. "I wonder if it's true."

"No one knows," Mr. Cain replied. "But several centuries later, here in America, one of the later Templars developed a perfect ruby-red rose in honor of the legend. Subsequently the Templar rose became world-famous and it's won a great many awards and prizes."

Cameron, beaming, interjected, "And I've had the privilege of tending them in the Winterfire conservatory these past years. I daresay they've suffered no lack of attention."

"You've done a marvelous job with them," Denise said to Cameron. "You should be proud!" Cameron smiled gratefully and went off jauntily to the kitchen.

The conversation drifted then to the astonishing fact

of Evan's safe return. "I still can't believe it!" Denise said.

Mr. Cain agreed. "When he called me just after he'd deplaned in New York, I was floored. It's the most extraordinary thing I've ever heard of!"

Laurel observed, "He must have arrived some time yesterday evening, soon after I arrived." Mr. Cain nodded. "I wish I'd known," she went on. "As it was, I couldn't help feeling awkward, being here."

"Eh? Why should you?" Mr. Cain seemed surprised. He was a dapper, neat little man with the brightest birdlike eyes Laurel had ever seen. She was certain those eyes missed very little.

"If I'd been forewarned, I'd have gone back to the West Coast immediately. But here I was, ready to pack up the Templar Papers and make off with them—when their owner appeared! Which made me feel like a burglar, caught red-handed." She smiled, then continued. "Mr. Templar expressed himself quite eloquently on the subject of *vultures* . . . such as myself."

"Oh, dear, there's something decidedly wrong here," Mr. Cain said, dabbing at his lips with his napkin. "I'm sure Evan didn't mean *you!* How could he? Why, we'd talked about your being here, and he'd already told me—" He broke off, listening. They heard the sound of the great front door opening and closing, and the conversation hung suspended. Laurel, certain that Mr. Cain had been on the brink of telling her what she needed to know, waited with the others to see who had come in. She heard laughter, footsteps crossing the black-and-white marble floor of the entrance hall, and the sound of the clock chiming ten, and then the dining-room door opened. Through the doorway came a woman of dark and formidable loveliness, smiling, her eyes bright. And just behind her, resplendent in evening clothes, also smiling, stood Evan Templar.

The rest of the evening crept slowly by, at least so it seemed to Laurel. Evan's appearance with the flame-like Charlotte—Laurel hadn't caught her last name—had effectively blocked the subject of the papers. No appropriate opening occurred in the laughter and chatter into which she could drop the all-important question.

They went into the den for coffee and liqueurs, and Laurel sat waiting, listening, smiling, and watching Evan and the woman, who sat close together directly opposite her. Charlotte had the kind of movie-star beauty that Laurel had always wished for. Her hair, as blue-black as Evan's, and as lustrous, was parted in the center and drawn softly back, held at the nape by a glittering jeweled clip and let fall in rippling waves. Her eyes were large, the color of smoke, shadowed with jade, slightly slanted, and black-fringed. Her mouth was very red and moist. She wore a royal-blue satin gown that must have cost thousands and come from Paris, and Laurel was certain that there were no copies of it anywhere. She had worn a full-length ocelot evening wrap when she came in, but now it lay where she had tossed it, across the sixteenth-century harpsichord in the corner of the room. Laurel was irritated by that, but she didn't know whether she objected to the woman's lack of respect for the priceless instrument or her offhand carelessness with the coat.

Watching the two of them, Laurel thought, He's drowning in her eyes, he hangs on her every syllable— and I wish I could get out of here.

But she stayed. She stayed until Mr. Cain had left,

and then Denise had gone home, and still Evan and Charlotte sat together, and Laurel realized that Charlotte had no intention of leaving. Laurel felt her face reddening as she rose at last and left the room.

As she climbed the stairs, trying to ignore the little, niggling upsurge of jealousy, she tried to avoid the direct gaze of the man in the portrait.

It was a long night filled with tossings and turnings and fleeting dreams that reflected the long day's emotional shocks and frustrations, and once Laurel awakened briefly to hear rain—*rain?*—thudding softly outside and slanting onto her window, making a sound like the crisp crackle of torn cellophane. She slept again.

Laurel had never seen anything like it—ever!

She had seen snow, of course. In the mountains, at Aspen, at Donner Pass and Squaw Valley, atop Monterey's Mount Toro, she had seen it and been enchanted by the phenomenon of wintertime weather. But she had never seen anything like this.

Snow that had fallen before she arrived still lay thick over the hills and trees. Icicles hung like frozen waterfalls from branches and from the eaves and windowsills of the carriage house. But in the night the temperature had risen above freezing and it had rained, and then the mercury had dipped again, so that the rain had frozen, coating everything—each separate tree limb, pine needle, winter-bare shrub—with an envelope of ice. And now the sun shone on it, and it blazed and sparkled, shining and bouncing and reflecting the light everywhere like millions of mirror bits, like frozen fire, flashing the sun's rays out in shards of bright flame. With delighted eyes she took in a fairyland world—an enchanted kingdom through which a wizard had walked during the night, waving a magic wand to create this wonder.

She hurriedly dressed to go outside. Remembering how uncertain she had been about the right clothing to bring, she was glad she'd brought warm, lightweight things; that was what the winter-sports enthusiasts at home had advised. She chose an outfit now, put it on, and looked herself over critically in the mirror. She saw a different Laurel Martin; this was a wintertime person! Still petite, obviously shapely in the clinging gold nylon ski pants and white sweater, but a different kind of person. And she liked what she saw. Her hazel eyes shone, her face glowed with health and anticipation, and she looked ready for anything.

She pulled on soft white boots, wrapped a gold scarf around her throat, and put on her quilted parka. Carrying her gloves, she left the room and ran downstairs. Near the bottom of the staircase she slowed and began to walk quietly. She had no wish to attract the attention of Evan Templar and his "friend." She hurried, tiptoeing across the entrance hall, and let herself out the front door as silently as she could.

Laurel took a deep breath and let it out slowly, gazing about in appreciation of what she saw. The air was surprisingly warm. The sun seemed to shine with many times its usual brilliance, for every ice-encased surface magnified it. Laurel had not worn sunglasses, and now she wished she had thought of them. She shielded her eyes with a gloved hand and squinted. The glare was ferocious. Now she knew what snow blindness meant.

Laurel walked away from the castle toward the mile-away iron gates, exploring, enjoying the morning.

From the groves and copses of trees came whip-crack sounds as the slight breeze moved icy branches. The brittle crackle sounded like firecrackers at times, and once or twice she heard a dull thumping sound. She could not identify it until she happened to turn around and look back at the castle at the right moment, and then she saw what made it; she was looking up at the castle's rampart and the corner turret when suddenly a great mass of ice-crusted snow let go and fell to the ground. The sound when it hit was like the reverberation of faraway cannon fire.

Laurel thought of the group she had met on the last leg of her trip, aboard the commuter airline. They had been students and others heading for a skiing holiday. She wondered where the ski lodge was. It must be farther north, she thought, looking about, trying to orient herself to the lay of the land.

The picturesque lane led her through a curved avenue of silver-white birches and thick green hemlocks, their shadows deep purple, the sun gilding the tips of the branches with dazzling lights. She walked on, following the lane through the trees and up a curving incline, and then she found herself on the brow of a snow-clad hill. Here there was a break in the trees, and she turned to look back across the rolling grounds at Winterfire. It stood proud and ageless, seemingly impervious to time, lovely amid its clumps of shining trees and bushes. The castle's windows caught the flashes of sunlight that glanced off the trees and ice-covered hedges, the breeze-ruffled shrubs and crystal-sparkling expanses of unsullied snow, and flung it outward, blazing. The fiery flares stabbed Laurel's eyes, making her blink back stinging tears. *Winterfire,* she thought. This must be why it got its name; the sunlight in winter makes it look as though it were ablaze. She would always remember it this way, she thought—and a strange lump came to her throat as she realized that she had quite fallen in love with the castle.

Suddenly she heard, or thought she heard, the sound of approaching hoofbeats. It was an intermittent sound, rising, fading, rising again, bouncing like echoes from somewhere behind her on the lane, an unfocused, disembodied sound made difficult to pinpoint by the same icy conditions that intensified and diffused the light and dazed her eyes. It seemed to come from everywhere—and nowhere. She shaded her eyes with her hand and looked about, seeking its origin. It grew louder, and she knew that the horse was coming nearer.

She was not far from the iron gates that marked the end of the lane. She peered through narrowed eyes and saw nothing, no movement there. The horse had to be in the lane she had traveled, somewhere between the castle and where she now stood. She thought it unlikely that Evan Templar would be riding through the open, snowy fields; they would be treacherous for a horse. Turning, she saw nothing; horse and rider were still somewhere in the wooded groves below the brow of the hill. She could not tell how far away or how near they were, but the sound of flying hooves now filled the air, and she moved quickly to get out of the lane.

She pushed her way through thick, snowy underbrush at the side of the lane. The footing was deceptive here; the frozen rain had made it slick. She saw that the side growth went down an embankment where craggy rocks and brushy stubble lay in deep shadow. She was off the lane and into this area when she saw the enormous black stallion and rider round the curve of the lane; there was plenty of room for the horse to pass. . . .

Her booted feet stepped onto what looked like crusted snow and abruptly, so quickly that afterward she could not remember the exact sequence of things, she slipped, falling on the solid ice; she screamed; the horse shied—and she felt the cold as her face touched the snow. Then there was a bright flash of pain as her head struck something, and pinwheels of colored light burst behind her eyes. She felt herself sinking into darkness.

Laurel became aware of things slowly. She was lying down; her head ached; the air was warm.

She opened her eyes. Soft dim light filled the room— her room at Winterfire. She moved her head and saw the antique satin canopy over her bed and the edge of her pillow with its embroidered emblem.

The sunlight had faded and now everything in the room was pale, the color of old lace. The drapes at her window had been partially drawn, but she could see gray clouds now instead of the morning's unblemished blue sky.

How long had she been unconscious? she wondered.

Then she became aware that she lay nude beneath the silken coverlet. Who had undressed her? And why? she wondered wildly, coming fully awake.

She was about to rise when she realized that someone was sitting beside the bed on the side away from the window, watching her. "Thank heaven, you're awake," Evan breathed. "Laurel, are you all right? How do you feel?"

She turned to face him. She saw tension in his face,

which was haggard with worry. His eyes were lightless. "Evan. I . . . think I'm all right."

"Don't try to sit up yet. Does your head hurt?"

Gingerly she touched a spot under her hair. "I have a headache. But otherwise I think I'm fine."

"Can you see? Is your vision blurred?"

"No. I can see all right." Laurel moved beneath the smooth satin and felt its sleek softness against her bare skin. "How did I get here? And who . . . ?"

"Do you remember what happened?"

"I think so. I was walking on the lane, and suddenly I heard the horse coming; I couldn't tell where it was until it was practically right *there,* and I got off the lane—and—I guess I slipped and fell on the ice."

"That's right. I had no idea you were out there; if you hadn't screamed, I doubt if I'd have seen you at all. You were very lucky, do you know that?" There was what seemed to be genuine concern in his eyes. "You must have been frightened. I'm sorry. But it never occurred to me that you might be anywhere near."

"I don't think I had time to be frightened," Laurel said. "Not for more than a second, anyway. Your horse is so big." She remembered the sight of him, a great black animal that had loomed up suddenly out of nowhere, looking as huge as a locomotive, and she was glad she *had* moved out of his path. "Do you always ride as though you were racing?"

The concern faded from Evan's eyes and something else came into them, something that seemed to say that he rode, and did everything else, exactly as he pleased —and that he was not in the habit of being questioned about it. He did not say it, but Laurel felt that he thought *she* had been at fault, certainly not he, and pretending otherwise was foolish. "I brought you in," he told her. "Dr. Grant has already been here. He said for you to rest; there might be a small concussion." He paused, his gaze resting on her face. "You had to be undressed so he could examine you, to be sure you hadn't broken anything. You hadn't." Then, more softly, he went on. "I'm to call him and report on how you feel. What do you want me to tell him?"

"Tell him I have a slight headache but really I'm fine." She did not ask who had done the undressing; she decided that she preferred not to know.

"I've been sitting here waiting for you to wake up. Thinking. Why on earth were you out there all by yourself? Why did you go wandering off like that?"

"Why shouldn't I? Did I do something I shouldn't?" Laurel's voice was cool.

"Yes and no. Ordinarily it would've been perfectly all right. But winter weather is tricky, and you're not accustomed to it. It can change within a few minutes; a storm can come up, and a person can get lost within a few yards of safety. You shouldn't have gone alone, that's all."

"I apologize if I did something that's forbidden by the master of Winterfire," she said, clipping off the words. She had suddenly had quite enough of his know-it-all, domineering manner. He was treating her like an incompetent child, and she resented it. She sat up, holding the coverlet under her chin with both hands. "I would appreciate it very much if you'd just leave the room. I'd like to get dressed."

"No, you're not to get up yet. Dr. Grant said—"

"Mr. Templar, I don't care *what* Dr. Grant said!" Laurel's voice and her temper began to rise. "Will you please stop treating me like . . . like . . ."

"Like what? How am I treating you?" Amusement

suddenly entered his tone. "I thought I followed prescribed procedure pretty well. A young lady who doesn't know anything about survival in winter climates goes out hiking on my property, panics, falls and hits her head on a rock or something. What was I supposed to do—leave you lying there in the snow?" He was laughing at her.

Laurel was furious. The ache in her head throbbed with her pulsebeat, and she glared at him.

"Laurel, *are* you all right?"

She nodded grudgingly. She turned her face away. *He* undressed me, she thought. He must have. Who else? Bridget? Denise? The doctor? *Charlotte?* No. It was this brute himself. This feudal lord.

"Can I get you anything?" he asked. "Anything at all?"

"No. Thank you."

"You don't know how worried I was, Laurel. You were so white, and you looked so fragile!"

"How did you get me back to the castle?"

He looked at her and saw the angry glints in her honey-colored eyes, and he smiled. "Why, I slung you over the saddle and galloped back. How did you think?"

"I wouldn't know," Laurel said. She keenly felt her disadvantage. She would have liked to whirl away from him, leave the room, get away from his antagonizing presence, but she had to sit there on the bed hiding her nakedness with a satin quilt, had to remain there helpless. How he was enjoying that!

"I'd like my robe, please," she told him. "I want to get up."

"But I told you, the doctor said—"

"And I told *you*, I don't care what he said!" Laurel exploded. "I said I want to get up! *If* you don't mind."

Evan sighed. He rose from the chair, went to her closet, and brought her fleecy robe to the bed. He bowed. "Is there anything else, milady?"

"No." And she added briskly, "*Thank* you." It was clearly a dismissal.

"Then I'll go and call Dr. Grant and tell him you're awake and that you'll probably live, out of sheer cantankerous stubbornness!"

Laurel's head had finally stopped aching. She had dressed in a soft pale yellow skirt and sweater and tied a blue-and-gold scarf around her hair. She had been about to leave her bedroom when Denise knocked at the door. "Would you like to see the papers?" Denise asked her.

"Yes, I'd like that very much," she replied. She thought that if she read the lord of the manor correctly, he would at least grant her that one small boon, and then she could tell Dr. Spence that she had seen the fabulous papers, even if they never got them for the museum.

"Mr. Templar, is it all right if I show Miss Martin the papers?" Denise asked him. He was in the entrance hall, headed outside, as they passed through.

"Certainly. You know where they are, don't you?"

"Yes. Do you have a key?"

"Not with me. Ask Cameron. He'll be happy to open the archives for you." Evan smiled briefly at both women, excused himself, and left. Charlotte was no-where to be seen, and Laurel began to wonder if she had been allowed to stay the night after all.

Laurel followed Denise to the kitchen, where Cameron was polishing silver and Bridget was making pies. Denise asked him for the key to the archives, but instead of giving it to her, he said, "I'll take you there. Come along." They climbed the staircase and went down a long, red-carpeted corridor with walls of stone and lit by small electric lights hidden in sconces.

At last they entered a balcony room, its three forward walls made of glass, beyond which the view of Winterfire's grounds, even in the sullen, cloudy light of the darkening afternoon, was breathtaking. "The room directly above this is the conservatory," Cameron was saying. "I'll show you the roses whenever you like. This is the solarium. The papers are kept in one of the rooms we just passed, but I thought perhaps you'd like to inspect them here, Miss Martin; it's more comfortable than the archives themselves. I'll bring the papers here to you if you'll be seated and wait just a moment."

Laurel smiled at Cameron and nodded. She and Denise sat at the long table near the west window-wall and waited. After a few minutes, Cameron reappeared, bearing a heavy bound metal chest, which he placed on the table. He produced a magnifying glass and said, "You'll want this, Miss Martin. It's easier to see some of the intricate work on the pages if they're magnified." He opened the chest, lifted out a wooden box, opened that, and spread his hands over what lay inside. "And here are the papers, Miss Martin."

At last, Laurel thought, excitement building inside her. To see them at last! She thanked Cameron again, and then, very carefully, touched the creamy, thick old parchment. It looked like alabaster, or thin-sliced, translucent veined marble.

The page on top of the thick stack of unbound leaves bore only one image: a ruby-red rose on a long stem with three perfectly drawn leaves and no thorns. The letter *T*, ornately drawn in the ancient Latin style, was intertwined with the rose. It was the same emblem Laurel had seen on the iron gates and embroidered on the Winterfire linens. "That isn't a part of the original manuscript," Denise told her. "The rose page was added a long time after the other pages were done. You're probably familiar with the history of the rest, but the rose is a later story. *This* page, the rose page, was done by an American ancestress of Evan's."

Laurel lifted the rose page out of the box and then carefully removed some of the pages under it. They were magnificent. The hand-inscribed lettering was surrounded by margins filled with illuminated pictures and curlicues, each page different. They had been painstakingly painted with tiny brushes in gold leaf and glowing colors that had not faded with time.

"You know, of course," Laurel said to Denise, "that the illuminator had to be very careful because not a mark of any kind could be erased from real parchment. So there was no room for error."

The other girl nodded, then studied one of the sheets and said, "The other set of papers, the companion set to this one, is still in France; it has thirty-nine illustrations of the castle there and life in the countryside around it as it was four hundred years ago—almost in photographic detail. This set is really supposed to go with that other one. I never found out why Sir Evan brought one set and not both when he came to America, but there must have been some reason for it. Anyway, this set gives the family's history all the way back to the Crusades, all the legends, all the who-did-what-to-whoms. Here," she said, indicating one of the pages. "This shows the bestowing of the symbols denoting that certain members of the family were Knights Templar during the Crusades, adding that to the family's coat of arms."

"They were Knights Templar?" Laurel asked, looking up from another page to scrutinize the one Denise held.

"Yes. The Knights Templar were the 'watchers,' the 'guardians of the temple,' during the Crusades."

"Yes." Knowing such historical legends was part of Laurel's job, and she loved the stories of the knights and their exploits.

"Well," Denise went on, "what about when Sir Evan had the quarrel with his brother, the duke? Do you know about that?"

"No."

"Then I'll tell you." Denise thought for a moment, and then said, "There were three brothers. One of them, the eldest, seemed to be a born villain. The other two were good guys. Sir Evan was the youngest. When they all grew up, the two older brothers both wanted the same woman—I don't know her name—and fought a duel over her. Sir Evan tried to prevent it and couldn't, and while they were actually fighting he rushed in to try and stop it, but he couldn't do that either. The oldest brother ran the other one through with his sword. That was when Sir Evan broke with the family and came to America. And took Templar as his name."

"Oh?"

"You see, up to then, it had been a title, or an honor,

because of the family's ancestors who *were* Knights Templar. But he took it for a *name*. He wrote that it was the only thing he wanted that was a part of the family's heritage, except the records and things he'd brought along with him. And his memories of the castle. So he proceeded to build his own version of it: Winterfire."

"That's fascinating!"

"There are legends and traditions by the dozen around here," Denise said, laughing.

Laurel, reminded of the current ruler of the castle, nodded grimly and said, "I know. I've bumped into one or two of them already."

Denise looked at her curiously, but Laurel said nothing more. Her attention was riveted to the ancient parchments. She lifted all the pages out of the box and laid them one by one on the table, counting them; there were exactly thirty, not counting the rose page. She studied them with awed scrutiny. She wasn't conscious of time passing, of the diminishing light as evening approached, of Denise turning on the lights and then later leaving the room. She was lost in the romance and wonder of the ancient pages and the stories they told.

The museum *had* to have them, she thought. She *must* get them.

But how?

She'd been wrong to think that Evan Templar would be generous. There had been no reason to believe that for a moment, and even if there had been, she had alienated him completely this afternoon.

But she wanted the beautiful papers for the museum! Nobody ever saw them here; they were kept locked away, hidden. They should be seen and appreciated by thousands of people! They should be shown in their own special room at the museum, even taken on tour across the country just as Dr. Spence had planned.

If only she could somehow get them away from Evan Templar. . . .

Night had come, and Laurel was still bent over the magnificent old leaves and their incredible legends when, without warning, Evan joined her.

Chapter Three

Laurel hadn't heard Evan's footsteps in the carpeted corridor outside, nor had she noticed the sound of the door as it opened. He was just suddenly there, looming over her where she sat, looking over her shoulder and then leaning down so that she felt his chin brush her hair.

He reached around her right shoulder and pointed to a small figure that had been drawn on the dexter, or right, side of a shield on one of the coat of arms pages. "That means whoever this story's about was the eldest son," he said. "It's called the file, or label. The second son's mark is the crescent, and the third's is a mullet, a five-pointed star."

Laurel looked up at him and nodded. "Yes." She was smiling, and he smiled too. How utterly different a smile made him look, she thought. When it was a real smile and not a sarcastic sneer.

He leaned very close to her, so close that even in the subdued light she could see the rise and fall of his chest below the deep open V of his shirt. She could smell the light surf-and-woods scent of him again. When she looked into his eyes she saw that there were little lights in their blue-green depths, shining softly. "Are you feeling all right?" he suddenly asked.

"Yes. I'm really quite recovered, thank you." And then she looked back at the page before her. "Evan, these are by far the finest examples of late medieval illustration I've ever seen."

"Yes, so the experts have said. Look." He pointed again to the page. "That's the sign of the seventh son, a rose. Did you know that?"

"I . . . think I'd forgotten it." His presence was distracting. She thought fleetingly of all the textbook facts she knew about heraldry and heraldic symbols, and then her thoughts sped to the last stormy conversation she had had with Evan Templar. Perhaps it wasn't too late to make friends with him, she thought. If she could do that, maybe the museum *would* get the papers after all.

"I came up here to ask you something," Evan said, moving around the table to face her. His light tone surprised her, and she waited. He shifted from one foot to the other, acting like a bashful schoolboy about to recite. He cleared his throat and said, in a self-consciously formal tone, "Milady, it occurs to me that my horse and I acted abominably this morning. We were quite inexcusable in our self-absorbed assumption that we had the whole outdoors to ourselves; thus it was our fault that you had to get out of our way and fell. And Sultan and I—that is, *I*—would like to make amends. So, since you are a guest in this stronghold and not a prisoner, and nowhere is it written that you have to remain in this tower room *or* below in the dungeon, I thought perhaps you'd consider going out to dinner with me this evening. Would you?" He cocked his head to one side, looking at her with an earnest, pleading expression. Laurel, still steeped in the mood of the old legends, thought of a dashing knight in armor being chivalrous to a fair maiden. And then she thought of a rakehell young nobleman dallying with a tavern wench. Which am I? she thought, laughing suddenly inside.

"I suppose I'd better say I'll go," she said, "lest you put me in prison. Or on the rack. Very well, I shall do your bidding, milord."

"Good! Now we're getting somewhere! You've come to realize your lowly place, my proud beauty!" His laugh was deep and carefree. "I shall await your pleasure at eight. It's just after six now. Does that give you enough time?"

"Yes."

Their talk continued in a light vein. It was a treat for Laurel, whose earlier impressions of Evan Templar had been so different. He asked her how she liked Winterfire, and she told him enthusiastically that she loved it. This pleased him. And how, he inquired, did she find the papers?

"I can't tell you how impressed I am, Evan. They're beautiful. And unique."

"Well . . . not exactly that. There's the other set, you know. The one that's still in France." He smiled. "Together, though, the two sets *would* be unique, a genuine treasure. There's nothing else like them in the world, never has been."

"You speak as though you'd seen the other set."

"I have. I went to the other half of the family's castle, in France."

"You went there? You spoke with the other members of the family?"

"There's hardly anyone left, just the present duke, and he's almost seventy. Impoverished. It's sad. The castle's gone downhill; it looks ready to fall."

"You actually went there! That must have been the first contact between the two branches of the family since Sir Evan came over here two centuries ago."

"It was. I spent almost a week's leave there, a year ago. It was like going back in time, looking into the past. I couldn't help wishing I could do something for the old duke. He's really a gentle, rather lonely old fellow."

"I think it was wonderful of you to go and visit him."

Laurel had gathered the papers together and now she stood up, meaning to replace them in their box, when Evan came to stand beside her. He watched her for a moment and then gently touched her hair, smoothing it softly; then he touched her face, turning it toward him. His eyes moved over her features.

Ask him now, she told herself. Now is the moment! Ask him now!

But before she could, he leaned down, lifted her chin, and kissed her. His fingertips moved along the line of her chin, caressing her throat, moving, touching, feather-light, where the little pulse beat in the hollow of her throat, and then, in one fluid movement, he drew her savagely to him and crushed her in his hard embrace. She was held motionless. He kissed her, gently at first and then with explosive wildness, his lips hot against hers. When the kiss ended he bent his head and kissed the hollow of her shoulder, touched it with his tongue, brushed his lips to her throat, and kissed the place just beneath her earlobe. He whispered, "Laurel, Laurel . . ."

Buffeted by sensations wholly new to her, Laurel could only catch her breath in short gasps and fight for control. Something deep inside her warned her to be careful of this man, warned her of the mastery she had sensed in him from the first. What he could not dominate by sheer masculine virility he took by pretending gentleness and charm.

Evan continued to explore her body with his lips and hands. His breath was warm on her skin; his lean body, pressing against hers, hard, urgent, demanding, created responses within her that went totally counter to her desire to wrench free and get away from him. She tried to think of Richard, but his image was lost in a whirl of sensation.

She could not *not* respond. Her mind wanted to call a halt, but her senses, awakened and ignited as never before, would not obey. She shuddered and leaned into him, her nerves taut and fiery, her breath quick and hot. She heard a low sound in Evan's throat, a soft groan, the kind of wanting sound a hungry animal would make.

And she drifted, holding him close, letting him touch her, until the saving thought came: Charlotte! He kissed her this way, he held her just this way. . . .

And then the anger came, and strength to twist herself free. She broke away, stood facing him as calmly as she could, her heart pounding, and raised her chin. She felt the sparks of anger in her eyes and knew that he must see them.

He gazed down at her, a look of molten desire in his

stormy eyes, and wordlessly, he turned and walked to
the door.

Holding it open, he turned. Husky-voiced, his words
like burning embers, he said, "Eight o'clock." His eyes
roamed over her body again, slowly. He repeated,
"Eight o'clock, milady." It sounded like an order, a
prediction of destiny, a challenge. And then he was
gone, leaving Laurel shaken and angry and afire—and
more confused than ever.

Laurel fully intended to avoid going to dinner with
Evan, even as she prepared to do just that.

Coming rosy and tingling from her bath, her hair
piled high and pinned on top of her head, she slipped
into her fleecy robe and slippers and considered what to
wear. She had brought only three long dresses—the
white one, a caftan more appropriate for a luau than
for dinner out on a winter evening, and the crimson silk
she had decided against wearing the night before.

She would have to wear that one, she thought. There
was really no choice. She couldn't very well go in ski
pants!

She dressed without haste, a part of her mind wholly
occupied with what lay ahead. A whole evening alone
with Evan Templar, it said; surely there would be an
opportunity to ask about the papers. All she needed
was one word, yes or no. But another part of her mind
looked on with stern disapproval. The man was a
monster. He was amoral. He acted as though he were
accustomed to having a harem, and she was merely the
latest addition. He was only doing it to amuse himself.
Why should she go?

But Laurel continued with her preparations, reminding herself that it was, after all, only a dinner invitation, and what could be wrong with that? A business dinner, that was all it was.

And he had been nice, she remembered. For a little while, he had been nice. . . . This dinner was a peace offering, a way of showing her he was sorry for the way he had behaved from the very start.

She raised her chin and decided that she *would* go. She would go, and she would find out what he meant to do about the bequest, once and for all, and then she could leave, with or without the papers—and that would be the end of that. She determinedly ignored the little voice that asked if she really wanted that to be the end of that.

She brushed her shining hair until it lay in red-gold waves down her back, molten copper on her creamy shoulders. She stepped into the flame-colored dress and fastened it, then straightened, smoothed the flowing lines of the skirt, and turned to find the red slippers that went with it.

There was a discreet tap on her door.

Laurel opened the door slightly. Cameron stood there, and she opened the door a bit wider. "Hello, Cameron."

"Good evening, Miss Martin," he said. "I'm sorry to bother you, but Mr. Evan asked me to check on something and report back to him."

"Oh? What?"

"Nothing at all, Miss Martin," Cameron said, his eyes twinkling. He nearly smiled, but not quite; his dignity forbade it. "That is, I have the information. The reply is crimson, the color of rubies. Please excuse me." And he turned and strode away down the hall.

Laurel looked after him, puzzled. Then she shrugged, closed the door, and went to the closet for the shoes. She had them on and was touching her temples with a light cologne when someone tapped on the door again. Mystified, she opened it.

"Again, my apologies for disturbing you, Miss Martin," Cameron said. "But Mr. Evan sends his compliments and inquires whether you'd care to wear these this evening. I believe they'll go nicely with the color of your gown, which, if I may say so, is exquisite."

Cameron's face was unreadable as he produced a small filigreed jewel box and opened it. Inside, shining softly against a dark velvet bed, lay three great teardrops of fiery red. "The Templar rubies," he said. He drew one out and held it dangling on a chain so delicate that it was nearly invisible. "This is the pendant. The other two are the eardrops. If you haven't chosen your jewelry for this evening . . . ?"

Laurel watched the great ruby as it turned, its facets reflecting rose-hued light. "Oh, Cameron, they're lovely, but I couldn't possibly wear them."

"Why ever not?"

"Because they're probably very old and valuable, worth a king's ransom."

"That's true. These jewels have been in the Templar family for nearly a century and a half, and yes, they're valuable; I've no idea of their worth. But it is Mr. Evan's wish that you wear them. That is, if you wish. And you'll be in his company all evening. What could happen to them?"

"Nothing, I suppose." Laurel looked from the slowly turning gem on its tiny chain to Cameron, who seemed personally eager to have her wear the rubies, as though he would be disappointed if she refused. She nodded. "All right, then, you've persuaded me," she said. She took the box from his hand, let him drop the pendant into her palm and smiled at Cameron.

"No lady has worn these for a very long time," he said. "You'll do them proud, Miss Martin." He bowed slightly, turned, and left.

Laurel held the antique jewels in her hand and wondered what this gesture meant. Was it another peace offering? Did he do this sort of thing—like that nonsense about the welcoming-kiss tradition—with every woman who came to Winterfire?

And then she thought, What would it mean if she wore the rubies? That his majesty had won his point?

She sighed. There was no figuring out what was in the man's mind.

They sped over the cleared road toward a destination Laurel could only guess at, for Evan had not told her where they were bound. Ahead, the car's lights illuminated the road and the snowy banks and evergreens at its sides, but everywhere else lay thick darkness. Snow had begun to fall lightly as night had come, and it floated lazily down in the headlights and great wet flakes of it smashed softly against the windshield. Evan drove well, watching the road but now and again glancing at Laurel, his eyes and his smile commenting much more eloquently than his words had upon her appearance.

She had worn the rubies, overruling her own objections. What harm could it do? she had wondered, putting them on. They glowed against her skin, enhancing its creamy beauty, adding to her loveliness.

And now she sat beside Evan Templar, bundled in a rich, deep-red velvet hooded cape that by its very simplicity added to the overall effect of her appearance.

Evan said, "If it were daytime, you'd be able to see some pretty country through here. This area owes its natural beauty to the things that happened to it during the Ice Age, did you know that?"

"I read something about it when I was planning this trip."

"The glacier came down, making all those little finger-shaped lakes you flew over and forming the valleys here." He glanced at her and smiled. She realized that his voice was full of love when he spoke of the land. Clearly he cared very deeply about it. This man was full of surprises!

"The glacier also formed the hills here. If you could see them, you'd see that they're oddly shaped; they're all oval. They're called drumlins. Some of them are quite high; some aren't. We're coming up on one of the highest now. It stands more than ninety meters tall, and the road goes right along the base."

They followed the long curved roadway that skirted the great hill that rose sheer and perpendicular beside the road. Laurel could see a bit of its rocky mass as they drove past.

They continued on, sometimes talking, sometimes not, and it was companionable and pleasant. Laurel felt none of her earlier exasperation in Evan's presence, and that pleased her. Lulled by his gentle manner, she began to let down her guard. Then she realized that this was the same overpowering, egotistical person; nothing had changed, except that now he was taking pains to be ingratiating. These were his company manners. Well, she wasn't going to be fooled; she'd keep in mind how hateful he could be! And after this evening was over, she would know what she needed to know.

"Look on your side of the car," Evan said. "There's a ravine that goes about fifty meters almost straight down. Another memento the glacier left." Laurel could see very little of it in the snowy darkness. "It's part of one of the ski trails. For experts only, of course. It makes a nice slope for jumping." He slowed the car momentarily, avoiding a patch of ice. "Do you ski?"

"No."

It was as though they raced through a world of black and white, a world devoid of people or scenery. Laurel finally asked where they were going. "To the ski lodge."

"The ski lodge?"

"Yes. It's quite a place, much more than just somewhere for the skiers to congregate. It's an actual inn; it has a restaurant that's famous all over the country, not to mention the finest wine cellar anywhere around. It's different, and I think you'll like it." He grinned at her. The dim light from the dash touched his face and lit his eyes. "I'd have taken you somewhere else, though, if there hadn't been all this snow."

"Oh? Where?"

"Why, to . . ." He paused, maneuvering the car around another curve. "Let's see. Where would you like to go?"

Laurel caught his mood. Something light had surfaced in him, something irresistibly contagious. "Paris," she said, laughing. "And Athens. And Baghdad. For a start."

Chuckling, he said, "Milady, your wish is my command! Paris, Athens, and Baghdad—here we come! Just as soon as this weather lets up."

They were both laughing as he drove up to the wide torchlit entrance that opened onto the lodge parking lot. The night was dark and cold, filled with snow and the beginnings of an arctic gale, but something about it had begun to be beautiful to Laurel, and she suddenly realized that she was glad she'd come.

"And so, this lady who later became my grand-mother decided that since she had no talent for paint-ing, as had the lady who'd done the rose page, she'd do the Templar rose in embroidery. And it turned out to be beautiful. It's hanging in the gallery; I'll show it to you sometime." Evan had been regaling Laurel with stories about the family's history and she had listened, fascinated. She was aware that Evan was no longer putting on his lord-and-master act, that he was telling her these stories to entertain her, not to show off. He *could* be fun, she thought, surprised. He could be really delightful!

After the main course, Evan said, "I've been talking nonstop about the Templars, and now I want to hear about Miss Laurel Martin. Who is she, what goes on behind her lovely face, and how did Winterfire get so lucky?"

Laurel laughed. He had said it lightly, his gaze roving over her features, light from the candles reflected in his eyes. "There's nothing much to talk about," she told him. "I'm not very interesting."

"It's dastardly of me to dispute a lady's word," Evan said softly, "but I can't agree with that." As he talked there was an animation in the rugged planes of his face, a vividness that gave it a sort of grandeur. Laurel noticed that a lock of his black hair fell forward onto his

forehead just as it did in the portrait, and there were
shadows along the lines of his jaw. He wore a silver-
blue dinner jacket that made his eyes look darker and
enhanced the little lights in them. Laurel thought of the
riding clothes he had worn when the portrait was
painted. Whatever he wears, she thought, he looks like
a king.

"So you won't tell me about yourself? You're determined to remain a woman of mystery?"

Still Laurel said nothing. She had the uncomfortable
feeling that he was laughing at her again. She glanced
around the room; the tables were all occupied. Many of
the parties were young, obviously skiers, but there
were also quite a few older couples who must have
come for the superb food.

Evan asked suddenly. "Who was the fellow who
called you the other night?"

Laurel's startled expression as she turned back to
him met nothing but idle curiosity on his sculptured
face. No derision, no sarcasm, only inquiry.

"So it was *you* on the line!" she said. "You gave me
quite a start, you know. I'd thought I was alone in the
castle, and then, hearing someone else on the
phone . . ."

"Who was he?"

"That was my fiancé, Richard Bellamy. He just
called to make sure I'd arrived all right." Why was she
explaining Richard's call to him? It was none of his
business! Flustered, she stopped talking and gave her
attention to her dinner.

"It sounded like he just called to needle you."

"Why? What do you mean?"

"Does he always treat you like that?"

"Like what? See here—"

"Like a child. Like a piece of his personal property."

Indignant, Laurel flared, "He doesn't treat me that way at all! Richard is very good to me!" She was about to add something to the effect that how Richard treated her was her business, hers and Richard's, and tell him what she thought of a person who listened in on someone else's private phone call, but his grin fueled her irritation, though he said nothing. "Richard is wonderful to me. He's—"

Lazily, amused, Evan observed, "You're quick to defend him. Does he need it often?"

"Of course not!"

Evan's eyes had become remote again. He sat silently, assessing her. "You don't love him," he said. It was a flat statement, not a question.

Laurel glared at him, her exasperation growing. "What gives you the right to say such a thing? You don't know him, you don't know me, you're hardly in a position to say—"

"Wrong." The single word silenced her. Outraged, she listened as he said, "I know, because I recognized something in the way the two of you talked to each other. I talk to Sultan with more love than that—but then, I *do* love my horse." His eyes were mocking now. Laurel watched him, furiously rejecting what he was saying. She saw his expression change, a shadow creep into his eyes. "I thought I was in love once," he said. "It turned out I wasn't, but it took a lot of time and a great deal of soul-searching to realize it. After a while I understood that it wasn't a broken heart that I felt, it was nothing but wounded pride. I'm older and wiser now and I know, if not what love *is,* at least what it *isn't.* And what I heard the other night on the phone wasn't love."

"You are the most utterly infuriating person I have ever . . ."

But Evan's attention had suddenly left her. He looked beyond her as he saw someone approaching. He stood, held out his hand, and smiled as a portly man came to their table.

"Evan! It's so good to see you! I'd heard the good news . . . welcome home!"

Evan acknowledged the man's hearty greeting and they shook hands; then Evan introduced the man to Laurel. "Mr. Andrews owns this fine establishment," he said.

The two men talked for a few moments until the owner left and Evan, apparently no longer interested in the subject of Laurel's fiancé, smoothly suggested they go down to the Cavern.

Laurel's irritation had hardly cooled at all. She wanted to refuse, to ask him to take her back to Winterfire, wanted to remain angry at him. But she held her tongue. "What is 'the Cavern'?" she asked.

He came around the table, held her chair as she stood, and then, his hand on her elbow, guided her out of the dining room, through the lobby, into a hallway, and down a flight of stairs. "This area is honeycombed with hundreds of caves, many of them quite famous. This one just happened to be here, so, when they built the lodge, they made use of it." At the bottom of the stairs, Evan motioned toward an open archway, beyond which Laurel could see little, for the lighting was dim. Music poured from the room beyond the arched portal.

Inside, Laurel's mood lightened again as she looked

about. The far wall, lit by moving colored lights, was an actual waterfall. The ceiling was thickly hung with icicle-shaped stalactites. "They had to remove the stalagmites to put in the floor," Evan told her. There was a small bandstand on which five musicians, dressed in jeans and ski sweaters, were at work, and along the wall on the left side stood an enormous cavelike stone fireplace, its mammoth interior blazing merrily.

"Let's sit over there on the hearth," Evan suggested. There were several couples on the small dance floor, and others at the tiny tables that were clustered together in intimate groupings on the far side of the room. Laurel and Evan found a place among the cushions on the raised hearth, sat down, and when the waiter came ordered drinks.

"It *is* unusual," Laurel said, but Evan could not hear her over the din of the music. He moved closer to her and brought his head nearer her lips. For an instant she thought he meant to kiss her again and she shivered, though whether with pleasure or fear she could not have said. "I said it's unusual. I like it."

He nodded, then brought his lips to her ear, so close that she felt the warm touch of his breath. "I thought you would."

Laurel felt her anger at him slipping away again. What *is* it about him? she demanded of herself. The man made her angry enough to explode one minute, and the next . . .

Abruptly, the musicians finished their song, and Laurel drew away from Evan in the sudden quiet. The group on the bandstand was about to begin another number, and the waiter brought their drinks. Evan lifted his as though in toast to her, but he said nothing.

The music this time was softer, slower, an oldie that Laurel had not heard for some time. It was a song she had always liked, a love song. Evan took her hand without a word, stood, and led her to the dance floor. He held her to him, covered her small hand with his, and held it against his chest. Laurel's head reached only to his chin, even though she was wearing heels. She looked up at his face, only inches away, watched the play of colored lights on it, and remembered that only a few minutes before his eyes had been cold, his words cutting and insulting. She tried again to puzzle out the workings of his mind. It was impossible. And little by little the music and his closeness claimed her attention, and she gave herself up to dancing.

Laurel had not danced so well in years, and now, moving in rhythm with the sensuous throbbing music, perfectly in unison with Evan's expert steps, she tried to remember how long it had been since she had danced at all. Richard never took her dancing, she realized, and it surprised her. What did they do? They went to lectures. And parties—*his* friends' parties. And his business get-togethers. Her mind wandered on, going along a curious new road she had not explored before. She and Richard didn't do anything that was just *fun*, she admitted to herself. They didn't really care about the same things. She tried to understand his work, but she didn't, and when they talked about hers, they usually ended up in an argument.

Could Evan Templar be right? *Did* she love Richard?

Held close in the arms of this dark stranger, Laurel moved gracefully while her mind dissected her relationship with the man she meant to marry. She felt the hard strength of Evan's steel-muscled form pressing against her body as they moved, felt the pressure of his hand covering hers, felt his heart beating close to her own, felt the tingle of his breath on her cheek—and she felt disloyal. And guilty. Richard had done nothing to deserve the things she was thinking, she told herself sternly.

Then Evan's hand moved on her back and he touched her bare skin and softly caressed it, and all thoughts of Richard Bellamy faded.

Evan bent his head to murmur near her ear, "Laurel, you're beautiful." He brushed a kiss on her hair, and when he drew back she noticed the little scar. She touched it with her free hand.

"What did that?" she asked.

"That scar? Why, that's a reminder to . . . mind my own business," he replied, laughing a little. "I got it one day when I was brash enough to take on the biggest kid at school in hand-to-hand combat. I was all of ten at the time."

So, she thought. The mighty scion of the Templar dynasty went barging into battle and got cut down to size! Good! That must have given him a shock!

"He was the school bully. That day he tackled my friend, who happened to be a kid about half his size, wore glasses, you know the kind—all brains, no brawn. I went to the rescue, and it ended up with both of us down for the count and the bully still cock of the walk."

"Oh."

She shivered slightly. He watched her closely, his eyes tracing the lines and features of her face again, looking *into* her, and she could almost feel the touch of his gaze. He felt her small shiver and asked, "Laurel, what is it?"

"Nothing. It's . . . nothing." But he held her more closely then, so closely that they seemed to move as one, so near that she was aware with every nerve of her body that this man, this strange, complex man who defied her logic and infuriated her and touched off emotions within her that she hadn't known were there, had some awesome power over her.

The music was ending. Evan executed the final steps of the dance and she followed him with practiced finesse. It was as though they had danced together for years. As the last note died away and the musicians announced that they were taking a short break, Evan and Laurel parted and walked back to the hearth. Her mind was full of him. Her body tingled and burned, her senses drifted on a tide of languor, her feet stepped without her volition.

When they sat down again, Laurel reached out to pick up her glass and the ring on her left hand sent out a flash of light. Richard's ring, she thought And then she wondered why it was that whenever she thought of it, she thought of it as Richard's ring, never hers.

"You dance well, Laurel," Evan commented. "You must do it a lot."

"You're easy to follow." But Laurel's pensive mood lingered.

"Why, thank you, milady!" he said, inclining his head in a gallant nod. "Flattery will get you everywhere." He raised her hand to his lips, again palm up, and kissed it softly, lingeringly. The feeling was maddening, sweet, wild. "Let's see," he said, lowering her hand. "Was that Paris, Athens, and Baghdad?"

"You didn't forget."

"I never forget anything important," he said, and there was a serious note in his deep voice. Laurel was again conscious of his way of meaning things other than what his words said. His eyes smiled at her.

Ask him, she thought. Ask him *now*. It's a simple question. Just say: *Evan, are you going to let the museum have the papers, or not?* And he'll answer, and that will be that. No more suspense.

"Evan," she began, looking up into his eyes.

"Yes, milady?" His smile was still there, deep in his eyes. He waited.

She said, "I need to know about the papers." She took a deep breath. Forming the question, speaking the words, was somehow more difficult than it should have been. "I realize you have every right to keep them. When your aunt made her will she thought you . . . wouldn't be coming back. The will is no longer valid, of course, and we've no reason to expect you to honor it. But I still have to ask, because, after all, that's why I'm here. So if you'll just tell me, I can . . ."

But Evan was no longer looking at her. He had seen someone in the archway leading to the Cavern, someone who had been looking for him. He waved and stood. Laurel followed his look and saw Mr. Andrews, the owner of the lodge, making his way between the tables and across the dance floor, approaching them. When he reached them Evan took note of his concerned face and asked quickly, "What is it?"

"I'm afraid I have some bad news, Evan," the older man said.

Laurel could hardly hear their voices—they had turned away, and they were speaking in low tones—but

she could hear snatches: "Nobody was hurt, luckily
. . . night skiers reported it . . . happens every year
or two . . . simply let loose and dumped tons of snow
on the road . . . avalanche . . . phone lines down . . .
won't be able to drive home tonight. But of course you
could ski it."

Ski it?" Laurel echoed as she moved closer, appalled
at the idea. Over terrain like a roller coaster, at night,
in a gale?

"No," Evan said, glancing down at her. "Miss Martin isn't familiar with the trails."

Miss Martin had never been on a pair of skis in her
life, Laurel thought. And Miss Martin had no intention
of putting on a pair for the first time *now!* What a
preposterous notion!

The two men's voices became difficult to hear again,
until Laurel heard Mr. Andrews say, ". . . stay here. I
have one room."

"Only one?" Evan asked.

"Yes, and there's that one only because somebody
canceled out this afternoon. You know how it is at this
time of year; we're always booked solid."

"Well, then." Evan looked from the owner's kindly
face back down at Laurel. A small frown puckered his
brows. "We'll just have to stay. They'll get the road
cleared tomorrow, wouldn't you guess?"

"Yes, I imagine so, but it was a pretty big fall, they
said."

"Thanks for coming to find us," Evan said. "I'm glad
you remembered we were here."

"I didn't think you'd left. I'm sure glad you two
weren't on the road at that particular spot when it
happened!"

Laurel heard the men as they talked on about the avalanche that had come roaring down off the tallest drumlin and covered the road where they had been only an hour or two before. But her mind was busy with only one detail: There's only one room.

Only one bedroom.

Chapter Four

The room was spacious, with a large braided rug on its gold-oak floor, Alpine pictures on the wall, and a dark, beamed ceiling. There was only one bed in it, but there was an oversized couch that looked ample for sleeping. Laurel surveyed the room warily, wondering how she would manage undressing, and if her long slip would do for a nightgown. It was practically transparent, but it was the only thing she had, so it would have to do.

Evan said, "I think I'll drive out as far as I can and see what the situation looks like. I won't be gone long."

"Do you think it's safe?" she asked him. "Mightn't more snow come down?"

"Would you care, milady?" His grin was teasing.

She turned away from him. "I only meant . . ."

"I'm touched. Tell you what. If I'm not back in half an hour, call Andrews and have him send out a Saint

Bernard." He opened the door. "It's probably quite safe, Laurel. Don't worry. I'll be back in a little while."

By the time Evan returned, Laurel was in bed. She tried to ignore the sound of his key in the lock and pretended to be asleep.

The room was lighted by one small lamp, which she had left turned on for him. Her face was in shadow, turned away from the door.

She had called down for linens and had the couch made up for him. There were extra blankets and pillows. Now he came quietly into the room, moved around, stopped—and Laurel heard the small sounds he made as he slipped off his overcoat and hung it in the closet. Then he removed his dinner jacket. After that she heard small rustling sounds and the noise of a drawer opening and closing, and then his muffled footsteps as he crossed the braided rug. The footsteps halted beside the bed. She knew where he was; she could feel his presence, hear his breathing. She knew that he stood very near the bed, looking down at her. Her heart skipped and hammered. *Go away,* she silently begged.

He whispered her name. She tried to avoid any response, but it was impossible. She opened her eyes and turned her head toward him. He wore nothing at all above the waist.

"Did I wake you?" he asked.

"No." She sat up, clutching the covers under her chin. "How is the road?"

"Covered by a pretty good load of snow. I couldn't see much, but it looks like maybe a hundred yards of road are blocked."

Laurel thought again of their having passed that point on their way to the lodge. Strangely, she felt no fear at the thought; she had been with Evan, safe and warm in his car. There had been no reason not to feel safe. But that had been then. . . .

She did not feel at all safe in his presence now, looking up at him, watching his expression change, reading the look that came into his eyes.

The hungry gaze that caressed her face was fiery. His body was outlined by the soft light of the lamp behind him; his face was shaded, and his eyes were like burning embers, pouring heat into her, searing her.

He sat down on the edge of the bed.

Wordlessly he reached his hand over and without haste took the covers out of her grasp. She made no move to stop him. He slid the covers back, exposing her thinly veiled body to the waist. His gaze traveled down the smooth line of her throat, past her shoulders to the rosy-tipped mounds of her breasts beneath the revealing garment she wore. One shoulder strap had fallen over her arm, and now, gently, he touched her bare shoulder. Then, slowly, his tantalizingly soft touch moved down to trace the firm full curve of her breast. Still she made no objecting move. It was not until he had pulled the slip away and bent to kiss her bare pink breast with his devouring mouth that at last she stirred into resistance.

She struggled, but he held her without effort, his dark head on one breast, his hands cupping her breasts, his tongue touching first one, then the other, with soft, quick thrusts. "No! Evan, stop!" she begged, but it was as though he had not heard her.

An agony of sweet wanting had begun to grow deep within her; rivers of fire coursed through her. Her gasping breath tore at her throat. "Please, Evan, no!" But he went on. . . .

He lay half on her, half beside her, his lips on her breasts, his hands teasing, the sheer overpowering size of him rendering her incapable of movement. Torrents of desire flooded her being. He lifted his head at last, moved above her to look down into her eyes, and brought his mouth to hers, open, moist, hard.

She struggled, trying to avoid his kiss, moving beneath him, trying to find a way to fling herself away from under him and out of the bed, but he would not let her go. Holding her with arms of steel, easily, he took her lips, kissing her until she began, against her will, to respond. Swept irresistibly along on the tide of her aroused emotions, she answered his kiss and pressed herself to him. He moaned, expressing his need in a wordless sound that crashed through her like lightning. He taunted her with his tongue, invading her mouth, and she let him do it, answering his probing, exploring tongue with her own. With mounting force he pressed his body to hers, moving against her, and Laurel, helpless against the onslaught of his power and her wild response to it, lay breathless in the bed beneath him.

Evan ended the kiss and looked down at her. He took her hand and slowly moved it downward. When she realized what he meant to do, she cried out and tore her hand away from his grasp.

He drew back, puzzled, and his eyes narrowed. "What is it? What's wrong?"

"Stop! You've got to stop this!" She pulled back as far as she could, trying to resist, to get away from him.

His expression changed to one of incredulity. It was as though she had struck him. "Why? What did I do, Laurel? What's wrong?"

"Just *stop!*"

"But why?" He frowned, his look intense and penetrating. "Are you trying to tell me you don't *want* me?"

"You must know I do. But, Evan . . . I—"

"You *what,* Laurel?" His face was still near hers, his look changing now to a questioning, bewildered gaze.

"Evan, this . . . can't happen. Please, you have to understand!" She paused, her mind racing. Evan's face took on a look as hard as flint and as chill as the winter wind outside while she searched for the right words.

"Yes?"

"Evan, I've never . . ."

His eyebrow went up and a small, unpleasant half smile formed on his lips. "Oh? You've *never?* Really? I wonder why I don't believe that."

Miserable, Laurel shook her head. Her hair shimmered in the lamplight as it fell about her shoulders. "I can't help what you believe. Just . . . let me go."

Disbelief, mockery, and something else, something deeper than anger, crossed Evan's face. He made a short little sound that meant many things, including derision and disgust. His face had become a cool and distant mask. In a low, rasping voice that set her nerves screaming, he said, "You play strange games, *milady.*" He stood up and turned away from her. He ran a hand through his hair, then turned back to look down at her with a narrow-eyed look that spoke volumes. "There's a name for women like you who—"

"Please, Evan."

"You got undressed and waited in bed for me, and you didn't mean to let me make love to you. Is that right?"

"Yes, but—"

"And you're a virgin. Right? Are you telling me that

the 'wonderful' Richard hasn't already taken care of that? You expect me to believe—"

"Evan, don't be ugly. Please . . . I'm sorry if I made you think—"

"You made me think a lot of things, Laurel. The way you looked tonight, the way you danced with me, the way you kissed me just now—what *would* I think? Listen, don't you *know* any better?"

Laurel did not speak. Evan stood staring down at her with accusing eyes. "You just meant to tease me and then shoot me down, right? Is that it? Do you make a habit of doing that to every guy who enjoys looking at you?"

"I don't know what you mean! Evan, I don't make a habit—" She broke off; the scathing look on his face stopped her, and a painful lump had formed in her throat, making it difficult to speak. She pulled her slip back up. Her head ached; her eyes burned with furious tears that she refused to shed. And then her anger flamed into being again, and she tossed her coppery head and lifted her chin. How dare he? she thought bitterly.

The calm voice of reason within her mind told her that she had been forewarned; she had known perfectly well what he was before she had chosen to come with him. What had she expected?

She slipped out of bed, then, remembering how transparent her clothing was, tried to cover herself with her hands and raced across the floor to the bathroom. She stayed there for a long time. At last she heard Evan's voice from just beyond the locked door saying quietly, "You can come out now. You don't have to be afraid I'll ravish you. I've never forced myself on a woman yet, and you're not likely to be the first. I'm not that desperate!"

Furious, she lashed out before she thought. "I'm well aware of that, Evan! You're probably quite well taken care of by the likes of Charlotte!"

Dead silence grew beyond the door. Seconds dragged by, minutes—and Laurel's agitation slowly cooled, to be replaced by curiosity. What was he doing out there? Why didn't he say anything?

At last, after perhaps ten minutes, he spoke again. He was no longer just outside, but across the room. "Come out anytime you like," he said. "I'm going to sleep; I won't touch you. Don't worry." His voice was so cold that it chilled her to hear it.

When at last she emerged from the bathroom, he had lain down on the couch, evidently in trousers and all. His face was turned away from her and his eyes were closed. Now *he* was pretending to be asleep, she thought.

She got back into the rumpled bed and pulled up the covers. There she lay awake, tossing, her head throbbing, most of the long night. Her thoughts were a torment; she could not control them, nor could she analyze them.

She still burned inside, wanting him. Never before had those feelings been awakened within her; never before had she even suspected that they existed. She thought of Richard. Richard's kisses and caresses had not been unpleasant . . . but they had simply never excited or aroused her. She had assumed that *those* feelings, those physical and emotional mysteries of which she had read and heard, came with marriage.

Now, torn between an acute awareness of Evan's

presence in the same room with her, guilt, and anger, she wondered if she had perhaps been wrong. Where did love fit in? Were love and this—this torment—two different things? Or were they supposed to be part and parcel of the same thing that also included mutual regard and compassion, understanding and caring? Wretchedly, her thoughts continued to circle, and she knew that she certainly could not think clearly in her present state of mind. She would have to try to figure things out when she had slept, when she was calmer, when Evan Templar was somewhere else and she was alone.

Once during the night she almost got up and went to him, but she did not. She finally drifted into a fitful, restless slumber sometime before the first faint light of dawn appeared in the sky outside.

Her dreams were filled with the wild, dark master of Winterfire. As she dreamed, she knew that she had stopped Evan not because she did not want him, but because she wanted him too much. Somehow, intuitively, she knew that if she had not stopped him, a part of her would belong to him always. She wanted much more than one night of love with Evan . . . even though her waking mind would never admit it.

When she awakened, Evan had gone. He had folded the sheets and blankets that had been on the couch, placed them neatly with the pillows on the end of it, and left.

It was a gray morning. No shafts of yellow sunlight came in through the window, but the sky was not quite so dark as it had been the afternoon before, not quite so full of heavy, dull-looking clouds.

Laurel was putting on the silk evening gown again when she heard a key in the lock and saw the knob turning. Assuming it was the maid, she fastened her dress and waited, but it was Evan who opened the door. Having bent down to lift a tray from where he had set it, now he came into the room, his face clear and friendly, his eyes bright. "Breakfast, milady?" he asked cheerfully.

On the surface it was as though nothing had happened between them the night before. They breakfasted together on the golden, fluffy eggs and crisp, fragrant bacon, thick, fresh-toasted bread and marmalade, and the dark, aromatic coffee he had brought on the huge silver tray. They ate as though they had been starved, and laughed, and spoke of the road crews and the downed telephone lines and the possibility of more snow that threatened in the sullen sky.

It was pleasant and impersonal almost to the end of the meal. Then Evan looked at her with those knowing eyes and said, "I'd like to issue a word of warning to you, Laurel. I've thought about it a lot since . . . last night. And if what you told me is *true*"—he looked the direct question into her eyes and she colored, but she nodded and returned his gaze—"then you shouldn't behave so . . ."

Laurel looked down then, into her cup. The coffee reflected her face and a bit of her fire-colored hair. Evan's words, and his look, embarrassed her. Quickly, embarrassment changed to kindling anger.

"I was pretty mad at first," he was saying. "But then I realized that if you really are inexperienced, maybe you don't know any better than to send out signals like that. Do you understand?"

She did not reply, only sipped her coffee.

He went on. "I don't know what kind of relationship you have with your 'wonderful' fiancé, Laurel, but all I can say is, he must be one cold fish! Hasn't he got any manhood?"

She started to answer, to defend Richard again, but thought better of it. Evan would only tear to shreds whatever she might say.

He said, "Let's have a truce, what do you say? I'll forgive you for getting my blood boiling—and you really did—if you'll forgive me for assuming 'facts not in evidence,' as the lawyers say. Agreed?"

Laurel was about to reply indignantly to him, but then, reacting to the word *lawyers,* she thought of Mr. Cain—and the papers. "Evan, I *have* to know about the bequest in your aunt's will," she said.

He laughed, and his eyebrow went up. Teasing, he said, "Ah! So it's the papers you've been after all along! Well, milady, I haven't yet decided about them. How's that for an answer? When I *have* decided, you'll be the first to know." He said it arrogantly, raising his cleft chin and looking down at her with a half smile.

"Evan, I do have to know. I have to leave—"

"Really?" he interrupted. "That's not quite the way I understood it. I thought you couldn't leave without either the papers or a firm no from me."

"Well, yes. . . ."

"Then, milady, you'll just have to wait until I get good and ready to give you my yea or nay. Isn't that right?"

Laurel nodded. He was right. He held all the cards. He would tell her in his own good time whether or not he meant to give up the Templar Papers, and until he did, there was nothing she could do but wait in suspense.

She did not remember until late that evening, back at Winterfire, that Mr. Cain had been about to say something regarding Evan's decision to give or withhold the bequest that night at the dinner meeting. What had Evan already told the attorney—when he'd first arrived back at home, before he had even met Laurel?

But she couldn't telephone Mr. Cain to ask. The snow crews had cleared the road, but the telephone lines were still down and there was no way of knowing how long it would be before service was restored.

And even if she could ask Mr. Cain, there was no guarantee that Evan hadn't changed his mind in the meantime.

Charlotte didn't simply arrive anywhere, she made a grand entrance. She came into the castle like a queen, Laurel thought, as if she owned it. Laurel tried to concentrate on the book she had been reading in the den, but Charlotte would not let her.

She came striding in, a bright smile on her face, and greeted Laurel lightly. She tossed her wrap, a cashmere coat, this time, on the sofa, sat down lazily, and crossed her long, lovely legs. "I hear you and Evan had a cozy little *do* last night," she said.

"How did you happen to hear that?" Laurel asked.

"Oh, word gets around," said the other woman. She studied her long, enameled nails. "I must say, I'm surprised at Evan. It's not like him to rob the cradle. At least, it's not like the Evan I used to know." She made it sound as though she had known him very well indeed.

Laurel said nothing, merely smiled briefly and turned her attention back to the book.

Charlotte said, "Where is our resident Legionnaire, by the way?"

"I don't know." Laurel had lost the thread of the

story and the words on the page ran together. Charlotte had shattered her composure, and she resented it. She closed the book and stood up. "Excuse me. There's something I have to do."

"By all means," said Charlotte, smiling her cool smile. "And if you happen to see my knight errant— and I do mean *errant*—send him down here, will you?"

Fuming, Laurel left the room and hurried upstairs. She went to her room, closed the door, and stared out at the snowy scene below. How could she stay on here indefinitely? Evan's maddening, arrogant refusal to give her an answer placed her in an untenable position. And Charlotte was infuriating. Yet what could she do?

She decided that she would wait only until the minute the phone was in working order again and then she would call Dr. Spence and turn matters over to him. He could send someone, or come in person, and deal with the situation that had developed. She would leave the instant she had gotten in touch with him.

The image of the woman downstairs rose tauntingly in her mind. Again she compared her own appearance with Charlotte's. And, as before, in her own opinion, she came off a bad second. Charlotte was not only beautiful, she was also the picture of poise and perfect grooming; expensive clothes only enhanced what nature had already given her. Her black hair glowed; her smoky eyes shone; her whole exotic appearance was striking.

It was late afternoon, hours before dinnertime, and Laurel was restless. She didn't want to go back downstairs, not if Charlotte was on the premises. Nor could she revive her interest in the book she had been reading. She was about to open her work journal to make an entry when she heard someone in the hall and crossed the room to open the door.

"Cameron! I'm glad it's you. I wonder if I could go and have another look at the papers?"

"Certainly, Miss Martin," Cameron said. He reached into his pocket to reassure himself that the key to the archives was still there. "Come along."

They reached the end of the long corridor and Cameron stopped at the door to the archives. Using his key to open it, he said, "Why not go ahead into the solarium, Miss Martin? There's really no place in the archives to sit comfortably, nor any place to spread the papers out."

Laurel walked slowly down the hall to the solarium, only to see Charlotte coming toward her, walking swiftly, with her large purse held tightly to her. Was there no way to get away from the woman? she asked herself.

"What are *you* doing here?" Charlotte demanded icily of Laurel, frowning, and then, without waiting for an answer, hurried past.

Cameron came out of the archives then, his hands empty, a look of worried bewilderment on his face.

"I don't understand this. I'm sure I put the chest away in its usual spot after you'd looked at the papers yesterday, Miss Martin."

"Why, yes, Cameron. I saw you go into the archives with it. I didn't see what you did with the chest once you were inside, but—why? What's wrong?"

"I'm not sure. I sincerely hope nothing is. But the chest seems to be missing!" He frowned. "Perhaps Mr. Evan took it. He was up here earlier."

They went into the solarium, Laurel leading the way.

She paused, breathing a sigh of relief. The papers lay spread out, not neatly, but in disarray and out of their proper order, on the long table. "Here they are, Cameron! Somebody else had them out, that's all."

"Thank heaven!"

Then Cameron frowned in puzzlement again. "But I'm sure Mr. Evan would have put them away. He would never have left them like this."

"Charlotte was just in here. I saw her leave."

"How odd! I wonder why she was in here—and how she got in. There are only two keys to the archives—mine, and Mr. Evan's." Perplexed, Cameron went on musing out loud. "Miss Charlotte's never shown the slightest interest in the papers before. Or anything else in the archives. She prefers things—expensive things—that she can use to enhance her own beauty." He caught himself up and smiled apologetically. "Forgive me, Miss Martin. I'm sorry. It's just that I can't help feeling a bit of . . . unpleasantness . . . toward the lady after what happened years ago."

"What was that?"

"I shouldn't gossip." Cameron idly picked up one of the ancient parchment pages. "Really, it's most unbecoming. And especially to a guest. Please forgive my lack of manners."

"Cameron, it's I who should apologize. For being nosy. I'm ashamed of myself." She was about to say something else but stopped short. Cameron's face had taken on a look of renewed shock. He had been shuffling the pages, and now he began to count them, carefully laying them one on another, his face almost frantic.

"They're not all here!" he cried.

"Oh, Cameron! Are you sure?" Laurel watched him anxiously as he recounted them.

They ran to the chest, peered inside, and saw that it was empty. "There are thirty sheets," he said, as though to himself, "plus the rose page. And now we only have twenty-six!" His face was stricken.

Laurel remembered the purse Charlotte had been carrying. It had easily been large enough to hold the missing pages.

The Templar Papers are no longer intact, Laurel thought, and the museum *must* be told, at once!

But why would Charlotte take those pages? What would make her do such a thing? Or did she do it?

Laurel reminded herself that what she had seen would never hold up in court. It was only circumstantial evidence. She faced the fact that she disliked the woman enough to think the worst of her and that was why she had jumped to the conclusion that it had been Charlotte who'd taken the pages. She *wanted* to believe it. It could have been someone else.

Even so, the question was still *"why."* What reason could anyone have? What purpose would it serve? Taking four pages of the thirty that made up the complete set, leaving a work of art greatly diminished in value—why?

And then, alarmed, she thought, Surely whoever took them wouldn't *destroy* them?

No. No one could be that pointlessly, wantonly destructive. What could possibly motivate anyone— She stopped abruptly as she remembered one important fact. There were two keys. Cameron kept one in his pocket. The other key was Evan's.

Cameron reported the facts to Evan at once, and Evan went with him to the archives and the solarium, and they searched thoroughly. They found no trace of the missing pages. Four of the priceless, beautiful, ancient pages of the Templar Papers were simply gone.

Chapter Five

The clouds parted in the west just as the sun sank below the horizon and sent long shafts of scarlet light across the snowy world. Rays from the day's last light flooded the den, bathing it in rose-colored light and outlining everything with red radiance.

Evan sat facing the windows, Laurel across from him, both quiet as the long day's setting sun sent out its splendor. Evan's somber face, morose and noncommittal, caught the fiery light. The beige shirt he wore took on the sunset's color and held it for a moment. The strange light transformed the room and then slowly faded as the sun disappeared.

Cameron came quietly into the room, switched on the lamps, and inquired about dinner. "I can serve it in here if you'd like," he said.

Evan said, "Good idea." It was the first thing he had said in an hour.

Laurel looked back out at the swiftly changing clouds in the west. The sunset's afterglow lit the long slopes and gentle hills, the evergreens and shrubs, with luminous beauty. The tips of the tallest trees on the grounds blazed gold for a few seconds and then dimmed. The shadows on the snow were deep purple, the open expanses a soft blue. Then into the still and silent scene beyond the windows came a movement in the snow; Laurel caught her breath and touched Evan's arm. Together they watched a majestic deer move slowly away from the trees, his great antlers catching the light. He took a few steps toward the castle, then stood as if frozen, scenting the air. After a minute or two he turned and went back into the gathering shadows.

"He's beautiful," Laurel breathed, and Evan nodded.

Evan had been withdrawn, lost deep inside himself, ever since the pages had disappeared. Laurel had spent the time in trying to solve the mystery of the missing pages; who had taken them, and why? Again she berated herself for having judged Charlotte on the basis of her own feelings toward the other woman. Charlotte had apparently left Winterfire immediately after she had encountered Laurel in the hall. As far as Laurel knew, Charlotte didn't even know what had happened.

Laurel's thoughts then shifted to her own feelings about the papers. She treasured them so highly and wanted them so much for the museum that she had, somehow, begun to regard them in some way as her own. That thought startled her. The papers belonged to Evan Templar, she reminded herself. She realized that they must mean a great deal to him. They were the actual records of things that had happened in his family long ago; how must the disappearance of a part of that priceless heritage make him feel?

She covertly studied Evan's face in the evening light and felt a pang of empathy for what he must be thinking. He seemed too far away, too immersed in his own private misery over the missing pages, even to be aware of her presence.

Cameron brought two hand-carved wooden trays with pewter handles, set up little folding tables to hold them, and went out again. He returned with napkins, silver, and their dinners. After he had served them he departed, almost as subdued as Laurel and Evan were. They began to eat in silence.

During the meal, Laurel tried to voice her thoughts to Evan. She said his name, and he seemed to come back from somewhere far away from her, reluctantly bringing his attention to her concerned face.

"I feel very badly about what's happened," she told him. "I don't know why it happened, or who was responsible, but I want you to know that I regret it very deeply. I think I can imagine how much the . . . loss . . . of those pages must mean to you."

A quizzical look crossed Evan's face as he contemplated her. "Laurel," he said finally, taking a long breath and letting it out in a sigh, "thank you; that's a sweet thing to say."

"I mean it. I'd give anything if this hadn't happened. It must be tearing you apart."

She was leaning toward him, her eyes soft, as she looked up into his face. He returned her solemn gaze for a moment, and then a trace of a smile touched his lips. Cameron came back in, saw that they had hardly touched their dinners, asked whether they had finished, and removed the trays.

Laurel was wearing the blue-and-gold caftan, its billowy silken material highlighting the amber-topaz color of her eyes and draping the soft curves of her figure. Evan continued to watch her, saying nothing, until Cameron had gone. Then he leaned forward and held her hands. "Let me explain something to you," he said softly.

She nodded. His mood puzzled her.

"I'm not upset about the loss of those pages for *my* sake," he told her. "I'm upset because of what this does to *you*." He paused, waiting until she understood what he was saying. "The papers are a Templar family treasure, it's true. Being what they are, historical documents that were so well executed in the first place and have been preserved so perfectly to this day, of course they're a special prize. And irreplaceable. But they don't mean very much to me. Aunt Dana was right; they belong in a museum where people can see them and appreciate what they are. I'd planned to give them to you all along; did you think I'd be rotten enough not to?" He laughed, watching as Laurel's eyes lit with joy. "But now, what can I say? This thing should never have happened. But it did, right here in my own home, where your acquisition should have been perfectly safe. Now you'll be forced to go back to the museum with a far less valuable work of art, one that's no longer complete. The museum may think it was your fault in some way. It's conceivable you could lose your job over it. Do you see? I'm concerned about this because of what it will mean to *you*."

"Oh, Evan! You'd planned all along to let us—"

He held up a finger to silence her and went on. "Now, what I've been thinking is this. I have a pretty good idea what happened to the pages. *And* why. I wasn't sure at first; I just couldn't believe that the person I think took them would do a thing like that. But little by little I began to understand the psychology of what motivated . . . that person."

"Who, Evan?"

"No. I won't tell you that."

"Well, then . . . knowing whatever it is that makes you think you know who did it, can you also tell whether the pages are safe? Would the person harm them?"

Evan gave a little shrug of uncertainty. "I can't say for sure, but I have a pretty good hunch, and I think the pages are safe. They'd be of no use at all if they were harmed or destroyed, but intact, they're a weapon. Or something to use to get something the person who took them wants. Something to barter with. Do you see?"

"No, I don't understand at all, Evan."

"Good. Don't try. Just . . . trust me. All right?"

"Trust you?"

"To get the missing pages back for you."

"Do you think you can? How? Do you really think—"

"Leave that to me."

"But . . . can't I help? Whatever you have in mind, can't I—?"

"*No.* No, Laurel! I don't need your help. In fact, that's just exactly what I don't need."

Hurt and rebuffed, Laurel sat back in her chair.

He said, "Believe me, you can't help. You'd only be a hindrance."

She bridled at his tone, which was condescending, final and arbitrary, as though she were a little girl to be

ordered about. She frowned at him. The transforma-
tion had happened again, changing his short-lived
gentleness to sardonic arrogance.

"I don't understand any of this," she said. "First you
tell me you intended to let the museum have the
papers, but now you won't let me help you to get the
missing pages back. You won't tell me who you think
took them; you won't even tell me what you're planning to do to try to get them back. Wouldn't it be
sensible for you to let me in on it? Isn't it at least
partially my responsibility?"

"It most certainly is not. And you mustn't interfere,
Laurel! It has nothing to do with you—not directly, at
any rate. Anything you might do would only make
matters worse. So just stay out of it; let me handle it.
And don't ask me anything more about it."

"Of all the arrogant, insensitive, utterly incompre-
hensible—" She broke off in sheer frustration.

His smile changed into the frosty, teasing grin that
never failed to madden her. His eyes traveled lazily
over the lines of her face, over her body beneath the
caftan. She could feel the anger growing within her. He
laughed softly, the derisive chuckle that he used to
assert, more clearly than words could say, that he was
the undisputed master here, the man in charge—and
that he was not to be questioned.

Determined to escape before she lost control, she
rose from her chair and moved toward the door. He
followed her with his eyes and she felt his stare. She
turned. "Evan Templar," she said, her voice low and
furious, "I don't know why I let myself feel one
moment's sympathy for you. You are contemptible!"
She left the room. The last word she had spoken hung
in the air like an explosion.

In the sanctuary of her room, Laurel paced for a while, unsettled, letting her anger cool. Then she undressed, drew a warm bath, and sank into the water. Idly, her thoughts drifted.

The bath oil she had added had a surfy scent. It reminded her of Evan's aftershave lotion, and set off a chain reaction of thoughts. Would she ever see a ruby-red rose again, she wondered, or a black horse, would she ever smell the ocean or a Christmas ever-green, without thinking of Evan Templar?

Images of his face followed one another through her thoughts. She saw him in her mind's eye as she had seen him in the flesh: brooding, his face dark, his eyes far away. Laughing, with little lights dancing deep in his shining eyes. Solemn, the way he looked when he talked about something that was important to him, his rugged features animated. Smiling, his even white teeth flashing, the small laughlines visible at his temples. Foreboding. Boyish, pretending to be bashful, grin-ning. And cold, aloof, lofty, and commanding, as she had seen him a little while earlier. . . .

How would she ever forget the man? Would his memory forever taunt and challenge her?

As she stepped out of the tub and dried off she asked herself what it was about him that made her feel as she did.

His ancient family heritage? No. She had met other people who had similar family trees, or even grander ones.

His fortune? No. Richard was quite wealthy too, and she had certainly never turned wanton at *his* touch!

The castle? No. There were quite a few castles right on the California coast near San Diego; she had visited some of them. Most were bigger and a lot more authentic than this one. No, it wasn't Winterfire.

What, then? His body? No. Lots of men had tall, lean, hard bodies that moved like a jungle cat's. Lots of men wore slim pants and open shirts that showed their chests, and danced well, and towered over her. His face? Craggy and scowling, dark, rugged, with a play of unpredictable emotions on it, and a tiny scar?

As she thought of that scar and what had caused it, Laurel again felt her anger melting away. No, the disturbing, upsetting way Evan Templar affected her was not due to any of those things. It was all of them; it was just . . . *him.*

She tossed her head and turned her thoughts elsewhere. How long would it take him, she wondered, to do whatever it was that he meant to do to get the pages back? He had ordered her to stay out of it; all right, she would. She would avoid him entirely since he was so high and mighty and didn't need any help.

But how long would it be before he either succeeded or failed in whatever he was planning? How long would it be before she could leave Winterfire?

She realized that he had meant to give the papers to the museum all along. That warmed her; he could be generous, she thought. And then it exasperated her all over again. If he had just told her that at first, she could have taken the papers, all of them, and gone. She'd have been back in San Diego by now, and she and Dr. Spence would be readying the Templar Papers for display. And this unexpected unpleasantness would never have happened.

Laurel dressed in Oriental-style pajamas and brushed her hair. The pajamas had come from San Francisco and she had bought them to wear at home, alone; their color and cut and the silky-shining fabric that accented her form when she moved pleased her. She had planned to go to bed and read. But once she had slipped between the sheets and opened her book, her thoughts and feelings prevented her from reading.

She had come to Winterfire on business, but with dormant, unsuspected emotions. Evan Templar had awakened those emotions, and there was no way in which she could undo that. They were now a part of her, waiting . . .

Suddenly she knew that the inner fires Evan had ignited would never be quenched until she lay in Evan's arms. And if not Evan Templar . . . no man.

That thought brought with it a flood of questions. What about Richard? What about her marriage plans? What about . . . love?

Love. *Love* was what she wanted. She had thought she loved Richard. Now she knew that she did not; somehow that realization had come to her unbidden, but clear and undeniable. Regardless of what happened between herself and Evan—even if she never saw Evan again—she knew that she could not marry Richard; she could not go on as his fiancée. She could not marry anyone feeling as she did inside.

She removed Richard's ring from her finger and placed it on the night table. Then she left the bed and went to the window. Nothing disturbed the silence below; dark clouds hid the moon, and new snow, light and gentle, had begun to fall.

In the shadows below, a lone figure moved from the stables. It paused and looked up at Laurel's lighted window and stood for a moment, watching. The man— for it was a man—held his dark head high, as though he did not feel the icy flakes of snow that fell. When

Laurel turned away from the window, he continued walking toward the back entrance to Winterfire.

A few minutes later Laurel heard a soft tap at her door. She crossed the room and opened it, half expecting to see Cameron outside, but it was Evan who stood there . . . smiling. A small shock of surprise flashed through her, for she had certainly not expected to see Evan again tonight—and now here he was, every trace of his earlier arrogance gone, his eyes dancing and warm.

"I was out saying good night to Sultan and I saw your light. Would you care to raid the refrigerator with me?" he asked.

Unaccountably, all of the angry, frustrated thoughts she had been thinking were whisked away as though they had never been. His smile was like the sun peeping through thunderclouds; it brought a kind of magic to whatever it touched. It touched Laurel now, and she could do nothing but smile back at him.

She turned to reach for her robe, but he shook his head. "You don't need a robe. Come on!" And she went, as happily and lightheartedly as if she had been waiting for his invitation. They went down the beautiful staircase, past the portrait, and down again, through the entrance hall and the dining room and into the kitchen. They laughed together because it was night, they were alone, and it was mad fun, and Laurel realized that she was hungry, starving in fact, as they reached the kitchen.

Evan rummaged in the cavernous refrigerator and brought out as unlikely an assortment of foods as Laurel had ever seen at one time. There was cold lobster, which he told Laurel Bridget had probably meant to use in a salad for the next day's lunch.

"She'll murder you!"

"Quite possible." He grinned, not at all penitent. She laughed at his amiable acceptance of his fate.

And there was shaved ham, and a delicately wine-veined cheese of which he said, "A friend of mine makes this for his own family and special friends. He heard I was back, so he brought some over." Deviled eggs, potato salad, a tropical fruit concoction. Evan set all this out on the trestle table and poured great mugs of milk and then opened a cabinet and brought out pudgy, cloud-shaped cream puffs. "Bridget makes these, and I've never tasted any that could compare with hers!"

They laughed and ate, the rather large quantities of food disappearing quickly. "Tell me," he said between bites, "what are the museum's plans for the papers? What's on the agenda for when you get them back there?"

Her face sobered. "We've planned a lot of things. There's already been a lot of publicity, in the newspapers and on the air. My arrival with them is to be covered by the media, and then there's a press conference at the museum, and later on we've scheduled an open house and several receptions at which the papers will be shown to special groups of invited guests—historians, art experts, museum patrons . . . and then the public will be invited to see them. They'll be on exhibit for several months, and then they're to be loaned to a series of museums across the country."

"I had no idea they were considered all that important."

"Oh, yes! This is one of the most exciting things the museum has ever done! We expect people to pour in to see the papers. I think there'll be a great deal of interest."

"Seriously? I can't believe it. Why? The papers are just old parchments, private family records."

"But they're so beautifully done! They're unmatched; nothing else is at all like them."

"Except the other set."

"But that's not really comparable. The other set isn't accessible to the public."

"You're prejudiced. The papers couldn't possibly be as important an attraction as you say." Evan laughed indulgently at her. It was the first time Laurel had heard that rich, deep laugh, carefree and full of joy.

Then his face sobered again. "So, the Templar Papers really mean a lot to you, right?"

"Yes. To me, and to the museum."

He said nothing more for a moment. His face had become thoughtful.

"What is it, Evan? Are you thinking of the four pages that aren't there?"

"No."

"What, then?"

"Nothing. Nothing at all, milady." Then he brightened again and grinned at her. "Since you're so crazy about old family relics and such, how would you like to go up to the archives with me and take a look at some of the other things that are hoarded away collecting dust?"

"Now? Tonight?"

"Why not? Who's to stop us?" He was laughing again, pretending to conspire with her. He said, in a low voice full of wicked meaning, "There's nobody here but us, you know."

Laurel was very much aware of that fact. She had realized it when she had first opened her door to him.

She nodded now, her face serious. He laughed harder, reached out and touched her cheek, and said, "You'd make a terrible poker player, milady. Are you aware that your face gives you away completely? It's like a wide-open window into your thoughts."

She flushed and looked down. He took her chin and turned her face back toward him. "I think it's lovely. There are far too many closed-in, locked-up faces in the world, Laurel. You're open, you're sweet. . . ."

She lifted her chin, moving away from his touch, and frowned coolly at him.

"What have I done now?" he asked.

"I'm not a child, Evan. I wish you wouldn't treat me as though I were."

He didn't respond, merely finished his milk and waited until she had finished hers. Then he gathered up the dishes, put them into the dishwasher, and disposed of the food they had not eaten. The quiet between them had become heavy with unspoken thoughts.

He took her hand. "Come along."

Reluctantly she let him lead her out of the kitchen. At the foot of the staircase, Evan let her hand go and struck an exaggerated version of the pose he'd assumed for the portrait. Now he looked up at it and mimicked the posture and expression on his painted likeness. "Despicable fellow," he said confidentially to Laurel. "Quite unspeakable. A certifiable cad." She laughed. "Of course that's only the exterior; if you dig down deep under that sadistic facade, you'll find a mean streak and a heart of ice."

Laurel's musical laugh accompanied them as they climbed the stairs. They turned to go down the hall toward the corridor that led to the archives and the solarium. Suddenly Evan's face grew serious and he stopped walking. He had reached into his cardigan pocket and now he frowned. "That's funny."

"What's funny?"

"I don't have my key."

"Your key to the archives is missing?"

"Yes! And I'm certain it was in this pocket. I was up there this afternoon and I used it then."

Laurel thought back. He had been wearing the trim-fitting jeans, neutral shirt, and blue cardigan earlier; she had seen him dressed in them shortly after they had returned from the ski lodge. The next time she had seen him he had taken off the cardigan. Had he left it lying somewhere with his key in the pocket? Had someone taken the key then, and used it to open the archives to get the papers? Or had he simply left the door unlocked when he had been there earlier?

Laurel watched him search his other pockets. The key was not in any of them and he finally gave up, shrugging. "Well, milady, I guess we'll have to forgo our visit to the archives, at least for now."

They retraced their steps back along the corridor, each lost in thought. Evan's preoccupation darkened his eyes. Laurel wondered again who had taken the pages—using Evan's key, almost certainly. Where was that key now? Who had it—and the missing pages?

They had come down the hallway when Evan seemed to dismiss his ponderings and focus his attention again on her. As they passed one of the closed bedroom doors, Evan said, "That's my lair."

"Your lair?"

"Yes. Would you like to see it?" He grinned innocently.

"No, thank you." But she *was* curious. What sort of

bedroom did Evan have? Was it full of antique weapons, animal skins, and the trappings of an ancient knight? Or was it some sort of sophisticated, ultramodern bachelor's quarters, containing all the comforts and luxuries a sensuous man might want to have around him . . . and his women guests? Without warning, the mental pictures she had formed on the night that Charlotte had been at Winterfire shot through her memory and chilled her.

Then she realized that they were at her bedroom door. Evan lifted her hands and kissed them both. When he raised his head, he looked intensely into her eyes, and she thought of what he had said about her face showing her thoughts. Wanting to escape the knowing scrutiny of his look, she turned away. She opened the door and stepped into the room.

Evan still stood just outside the door. If she closed the door now, she would have to close it in his face. She turned back toward him, stood just inside the open doorway looking up at him, and said, "Good night, Evan. I had fun. I hope you find your key."

He nodded, but still he did not move.

She continued to look up into his rugged face, his eyes. His lean, sinewy shoulders were straining the soft cloth of his shirt. Knowing that she was making a mistake, but doing it anyway, she took a small step that brought her closer to him. In his eyes she saw the reflection of her own look of silent wanting.

This time the kiss was slow in coming. It began in Evan's eyes, and she knew it would happen and she wanted it to. Slow fire kindled inside her. Slowly she went into his arms, and he held her there close against him for long, long seconds, searching her face with his burning gaze, his eyes rapt, his arms hard but gentle about her. He bent forward and touched her forehead with his lips, kissed her closed eyes, her cheeks. When she thought she could bear it no more, his lips lightly brushed her parted lips, and it was like the feather-soft touch of a flower petal, yet as wild as a winter storm. Laurel's body tingled and trembled, the pent-up waiting fire about to burst forth. When his lips continued to hover, barely touching hers, the feeling built and built . . . and then he suddenly crushed her to him and brought his mouth down hard on hers. She heard the sharp intake of his breath as the onslaught of desire came crashing and flooding and exploding through her. It was a tidal wave of passion that gripped them both. He kissed her for a long time, his mouth persuading hers to open, his tongue teasing hers, his breath warm, fanning eddies of fire along her nerves. He bent her pliant body so that it met and pressed against his as he held her. She had no clear thoughts, only the wild, primeval urge that thundered in her pulses and roared through her whole being. Gone were her anger, her determination to avoid him. Nothing remained but the overpowering need to be loved completely by Evan Templar.

Evan ended the kiss without haste, then bent down and lifted her up in his arms. He carried her across the floor of her bedroom and laid her down on the bed. He himself stood erect, his expression fierce with smoldering desire, his shoulders outlined in the soft light.

Slowly he sat down on the edge of the bed and gazed down at her. He did not touch her. She waited, wanting him, as the moments lengthened. She looked up at him with an expression of yearning, of trust, of open and unashamed desire.

Equally slowly he moved away from her and stood

up. It was obvious that the movement required all his strength and determination. He shook his head. "No, Laurel."

"Evan?"

He stood by the bed again, this time looking down at her with hunger in his eyes, but also denial. "Not this way," he said.

"What's wrong, Evan? What is it? Did I do something?"

"No." He tore his gaze from her and walked to the window. He stood looking out at the scene below, the snow that silently fell, the darkness. He said, "You told me not to treat you like a child. I don't want to treat you like a child, Laurel. I want to treat you like a woman. But . . ."

"But what, Evan?" She sat up now, watching him, bewildered.

He looked back at her from where he stood, apparently trying to make up his mind what to say to her. Then he happened to glance at the night table, where the ring she had removed from her left hand still lay. Evan's eyebrow went up and a curious look crossed his face. "What's this? You've taken Mr. Wonderful's ring off? Do you do that often?"

"No. I . . . never took it off before. I—"

"Better put it back on, Laurel," he interrupted.

She gazed at him, utterly bewildered. "No," she said at last. "I . . . I'm no longer going to wear it."

Something almost cynical came into Evan's eyes. "Well, well," he said. "Did you decide that all by yourself—or did I have something to do with it?"

She flushed with anger and stood up, her body rigid and straight. "Please get out of here," she said, her voice husky with fury.

Slowly he crossed the room, looking at her with something unreadable in his eyes, the little muscles of his jaw flexing. He opened the door without another word and left the room, closing the door smartly behind him.

The things he had said and done troubled Laurel, but it was the things he had not said and had not done that disturbed her even more. Nothing about him made sense! She would *never* understand Evan Templar.

It was a long while before she slipped into a restless, tossing sleep.

Chapter Six

Laurel had seen several skiers flying by the library windows and had gone to stand by the glass to watch them. They moved swiftly across the rolling grounds, seemingly without effort. She was unaware of Evan's presence until he spoke from just behind her; she jumped at the sound of his voice. "Looks as though the new snow improved the surface," he said.

Laurel knew next to nothing about skiing, except that it looked like fun. Evan nodded toward the outside, where the skiers were racing each other, brightly colored splashes on the monotone of white. "They've cross-countried over from the lodge," he said. Then, looking down at Laurel and smiling, he asked, "Would you like to have a go at it?"

"Oh, no, I think not," she demurred. "I've never tried it. I don't know anything about it."

But Evan had left her side, ignoring what she said.

Over his shoulder he said, "Go get something else on and we'll go out."

So there was nothing for her to do but climb the stairs to her room and change from the heather-colored woolen outfit she had on into soft lightweight thermal underwear, warm socks, and the ski pants and sweater she had bought on the advice of friends. She took the parka along and went back downstairs to find Denise and Evan in conference just inside the entrance hall. She saw a pile of alien-looking contraptions stacked there: poles with wheellike things on one end, goggles, furred mittens, and skis. Evan was saying, "Hope the boots fit! Thanks a lot, Denise."

"You're welcome," Denise replied. Seeing Laurel, she said, "I hope you'll like skiing. It's really fun, once you get the hang of it "

Laurel learned the fundamentals quickly. Evan told her that the diagonal stride was the basic movement in cross-country skiing and then demonstrated it. Soon she was thrusting one leg back, gliding forward on the other, using her poles properly and beginning to move in the direction she intended, skimming along with a sense of exhilaration.

Evan assumed the role of instructor with seriousness. He went into detail in explaining the differences between Alpine, Nordic, cross-country, and freestyle skiing, described fall lines, moguls, and schussing, and not only did he describe these things, he made Laurel memorize them and repeat them back to him. He made particularly sure that she learned the meaning of the colors of the pennants that were placed at regular intervals along the ski trails so that she would recognize which ones designated the easy trails, for beginners, and which the trails for more advanced skiers and experts only. She wondered why she should learn all this, since she wouldn't be there long enough to need to know these things, nor would she be skiing alone. And it was highly unlikely that she would ever ski again, once she had left Winterfire. But she listened anyway, watching Evan's face as he talked, imitating the moves he made, and dutifully repeating what he told her.

"This trail we're on is an easy one," he said, pointing to the smooth, almost level course ahead of them. "But down the line a bit it intersects with a more difficult one; you have to know the pennant colors so you'll know which way to go."

Time flew by. Laurel was not conscious of the passing hours, the cold, her protesting muscles, or of anything but Evan's nearness, his grace, the look of his tall, hard body at ease, so at home on skis, and his deep voice talking to her about skiing as though they would be doing it together forever. Once she made too ambitious a turn, became unbalanced, and fell, landing in a tangle of skis and poles in the snow. Evan laughed and helped her up, brushed snow from her pants, and said, "You made a sitzmark."

"A what?"

"A sitzmark, milady."

Laurel burst into laughter. "What a word! Does it mean what it sounds like?"

"Precisely. Eloquent, isn't it? It means the impression made by a fallen skier . . . usually when he sits."

Laughing, they continued onward, hardly noticing as they skied farther and farther from Winterfire and the day changed from sunny to blue-gray under a clouded afternoon sky. Absorbed in the effort of learning to handle herself on skis and the increasing ease of it, Laurel hardly glanced at the sky until the sun came out,

spectacularly, at one point, casting yellow light on the
vast expanse of snow around them, creating vivid blue
shadows. They were traveling across gently sloping
fields of unbroken snow now, and Evan pointed out
several tall drumlins in the distance, their odd shapes
violet in the strange light. "Just over behind them is
where the avalanche was," he said.

The sky was filled with low-flying snow clouds,
though there was a break through which the sun shone.
Suddenly new flakes of snow began to drift downward,
and Laurel was again treated to a display of winter
magic such as she had never seen before. Some trick of
prismlike crystals, some sun-and-moisture phenomenon, gave the falling snowflakes color, and as they
materialized in the sunlight, twinkling downward and
seeming to vanish, they looked like jewels. It was as
though they stood in a field of white onto which
emeralds and rubies, amethysts and moonstones,
rained in a shower of radiance. Laurel cried out in
delight and held her face up to be touched by the cool
falling gems, and felt them turn from little icy stings to
warm teardrops on her skin. She turned to Evan,
laughing, her eyes behind the snow goggles bright with
joy, but he was not smiling. He too saw the sky and the
clouds and the strange new snow, and he knew their
meaning. They had come too far, it was growing late,
and there was going to be a swift and probably nasty
change in the weather—immediately. He spoke softly
and smiled so as not to alarm her. "I guess we'd better
start back."

Obediently, Laurel nodded, still enchanted by the
flakes drifting down. And then, quickly, the colors
were gone, the sun was swallowed up behind massive

sullen clouds again, and the wind awoke, grumbling. Evan asked, "Can you follow me? It'll be easier for me to go ahead of you."

"Yes, if you don't go too fast," she said. Confident of her budding skill at skiing, she assumed the stance and posture to begin, and he started out ahead. "How far is it? How far have we come?" she called, but he did not answer.

As they moved, the sky darkened further, and now the snowflakes were blue-cold and thick, falling fast and heavy. Laurel struggled to keep up with Evan. He glanced back now and then, never getting too far ahead, but even so, at times his dark-clad figure looked as though an airbrush had sprayed obscuring white paint between them, and even though he was only a few yards ahead, she was beginning to tire, so that it became harder for her to maintain the pace he set. She kept her eyes fixed on him, trying to keep up, determined not to let the distance between them lengthen. She would not slow him down; she would not lag behind. . . .

The wind rushed and breathed and then roared, and they were skiing right into it, so that she could not balance well as it changed its velocity. It gusted fiercely and the air was filled with swirling snow that obscured everything. With a flash of apprehension Laurel thought of the avalanche, but she saw no towering hills nearby from which another such could descend upon them. There were only the whipping snow-laden trees and the darkening gray sky.

Then Laurel remembered that Evan had told her that the area through which they now moved was honeycombed with caverns under its smooth surface. Did he know where they all were? she wondered alarmed. Did they all have visible openings? Were they like caves—or pits?

Up ahead, Evan turned, planted his ski poles in the snow, cupped his gloved hands around his mouth, and called out something she did not hear. The words were snatched away by the wind. It could have been anything. She tried to signal him that she had not heard, but before she could, to her horror, he had turned again—and gone on ahead at a much greater speed than before!

His movements had been so swift, and the snow so thick, that she had lost him; within seconds his dark figure had simply disappeared. The concealing snow whipped and drifted in eddies created by the chopping wind, wind that obscured Evan's ski tracks and left Laurel as lost as if he had never been there at all. She was alone in the screaming gale.

She planted her ski poles in the snow, breathed deeply, and steeled herself against the panic that threatened to overcome her. She reminded herself of the things Evan had taught her about safety and survival in winter weather. She looked right, then left, behind her, then straight ahead. There were no discernible landmarks; there was nothing even to mark the spot where Evan had been just before he had vanished.

She told herself to go slowly, conserve her energy, breathe deeply, take one step and then another. She ordered herself to stay calm, *not* to fall down, to remember that panic was the enemy, even more than the sudden storm. Survival depended upon keeping her wits about her.

And then she thought again of the caverns, and in a

moment's wild fright she was sure that Evan had
stumbled and fallen down into one of them. Of course!
she thought. He would never deliberately go off and
leave a novice alone in a gale!

She stopped and peered about, trying to see through
the thick snow where the opening of a cavern might be.
She saw nothing. But she knew, now, that that was
what had happened, and she knew in the same instant
that she must somehow get help. She had to get
people—in the ski rescue team at the lodge, somebody.

Blindly, fearful now for Evan's safety, Laurel skied
on, taking the route she judged to be a part of the easy
trail they had been on, for she knew that if she strayed
from it she would indeed be lost and Evan might never
be found—nor herself. The trail would eventually lead
her to the lodge. As she went she kept repeating over
and over in her mind what Evan had told her about
blizzard survival. "A storm can come up out of nowhere at a moment's notice," he had said. "Just keep
your head, keep moving, and try to reckon without
anxiety." All well and good, she thought, except that
her concern now was for Evan. Had he been hurt? Was
he even now lying in some hidden cavern, unconscious?
She prayed that he was uninjured, that whatever cave
he had fallen into was a shallow one, and that she could
bring rescue personnel back to the spot without getting
lost. What about frostbite? she wondered. She hoped
the rescue teams carried first-aid equipment with them.

Doggedly, moving cautiously, Laurel made her way
toward what she thought was the lodge's location. She
had become increasingly aware of the power of the
chilling wind. It lashed her mercilessly, blowing snow
almost horizontally now. Her muscles ached. She

forced herself onward, ignoring her cramping legs, telling herself that she would not succumb to the cold or the wind or fear. . . .

Finally she saw a pennant in the snow ahead. Her heart leaped. It meant that she was, at least, on one of the trails. The snow blotted out the color until she was nearer to it, and then, despairingly, she saw that it marked one of the difficult trails, trails that were for expert skiers only.

Now what could she do? She had to find help for Evan, but she couldn't ski this trail. She knew that if she tried it she would almost certainly fall or become lost and no one would know of Evan's plight. Or her own.

The wind, savage now, blasted like something alive and furious against her small body. Bits of icy snow scalded and stung her face and froze on the goggles. Awkwardly, she turned, her muscles protesting, her skis heavy with freezing snow. Her progress was agonizingly slow; inch by inch, it seemed, she made her way back to where she thought she had last seen Evan. She would try to orient herself and find the easy trail, then begin again. It couldn't be more than a mile or two to the lodge. She would find it and get help.

But there, looming up out of an almost solid wall of gale-driven snow, something—something houselike and dark and real—blocked her way. A structure of some kind! A shelter!

Moving toward it, peering through the icy goggles, she saw at last what it was. It was a cabin!

And standing in the shelter of its bulk, near the door, about to turn on his skis and surrounded by a nimbus of wildly swirling snow, stood Evan!

Now the tears came. Tears of relief, of fatigue, of

lifted fear and exhaustion, spilled down Laurel's face, coursed under the goggles, and made rivulets that fell and froze in the snow.

"Laurel!" Evan shouted, and now she heard him clearly. As he shouted her name he started toward her. "You shouldn't have followed! I was coming right back for you!"

Slowly she made her way to meet him. She could barely see. The snow and her tears obscured her vision.

"I wanted to get over here fast to see if this cabin was still here," Evan shouted over the wind. "It's a port in a storm, and we need one pretty badly just now. This blizzard may go on all night." He had reached her and now he saw her tears. "You're chilled; come on, let's get inside. I'll build a fire."

Holding her close to his side, he led her to the door, helped her off with her skis, took off his own, and then guided her into the chilly, dark cabin. He explained, "This cabin was my father's. He built it for what he called his hunting trips, but he never hunted anything, except with a camera. I think he just liked to get away from everything now and then. It was his retreat, I guess. It looks like nobody's been here for a long time."

Inside, Evan removed the goggles from Laurel's chilled face, smoothed away her tears, and took the cap from her head. Her hair fell in silken ripples over his fingers, and he smoothed it softly. "You're frozen," he said, looking deep into her still-swimming eyes. He caught her in a great hard bear hug, strained her against him, and brushed kisses on her cold cheeks. He said, "You're pretty good for a beginner at this skiing business. I didn't think you'd try to follow me, after I told you not to." He lifted her chin with his hand and brought his mouth down on hers, gently, and the chill went away from her lips; her heart skipped and hammered, its beat taking on a new rhythm as the kiss went on. Outside, the wind moaned and screamed in its potent fury and the snow swirled and drifted, and still the kiss went on and on—until at last they parted and Evan stood looking down at her, still holding her, and said, "Yes. To all the other lovely things about milady, add the fact that she's a pretty fair skier after just one lesson. But why *did* you follow me? I thought I'd warned you about taking chances in weather like this. You could have lost sight of me, become confused. You could have gotten lost, Laurel. Didn't you know that?"

"I didn't follow you! I didn't even hear what you said back there! I was afraid something had happened to you!" she said. "Oh, Evan, you're all right!"

Evan dropped his arms to his sides and stared at her. "You . . ."

"I went wandering all over, looking for you, trying to find a trail I could follow to get help. I thought you'd fallen into a cavern! I just happened to come this way and find you!"

Evan's astonished gaze turned hard at her words. "I can't believe it! You didn't pay the slightest attention to anything I told you! Do you think I was telling you all that about blizzards to *entertain* you? Don't you know how dangerous—"

Anger flashed through her at his misunderstanding of what she had suffered, and why. She drew away from him and tossed her hair. "I heard what you told me," she interrupted. "I listened carefully. I probably survived because of it. But I am trying to tell you *now*, Evan Templar, that I did *not* hear whatever it was that you shouted back to me out there, just before you disappeared. And I was afraid—for you. And I was trying to get help—for you." She frowned at him, her eyes flashing with anger. "I only found you by the sheerest chance. It's a wonder I'm not still out there looking for you—and freezing! And all you can think to do is berate me for not following your instructions!"

"Laurel . . . !"

Her eyes blazed. "You *assumed* I'd heard you. But I didn't. How was I to know what you'd said? I didn't know about this cabin or where you'd gone! All I knew was that you'd just suddenly vanished, and since *I* assumed you wouldn't do that deliberately, it had to have been because you'd fallen into a cavern or something. Nobody would go off and leave a person who's only begun to learn to ski out in such a storm. *Nobody* would do a thing like that!"

"But I thought you'd heard me and understood!"

"Well, I didn't!"

Anger had begun to show in Evan's eyes, too. Laurel saw it and did not care. She was shaking, partly from the cold and partly from her ordeal, but mostly because she was furious with Evan. "I was frightened for you, and I can't imagine why! But at the time I stupidly cared what had happened to you. I should have known better! All you want to do is reprimand me as if I'm a child."

"*Reprimand* you? I ought to do a lot more than that! You could have been lost—within yards of this very cabin! You don't know this weather! You've got to learn to survive in it!"

Thoroughly angry now, Laurel shot back at him, "No, I don't. There's not much snow in San Diego, Mr.

Templar. And that's exactly where I'm going the very
instant I *can*. So you don't have to worry about my
survival. *Or* how well I can follow your instructions."

Evan's face was a study in barely contained violence.
"So, you're going back to Mr. Wonderful. Of the San
Diego Wonderfuls . . ."

"That's enough." She rubbed her hands together and
hugged herself. She moved about to try to warm
herself. Suddenly the absurdity of the situation occurred to her; here they were, miraculously safe from
the howling gale outside, and all they could do was
fight!

But she could be as stubborn as he could. She would
not say a word or make a move to end the wretched
argument. He had turned away from her, and she was
too exhausted to want to do anything but sit somewhere
and, if possible, get warm. Her ordeal in the storm had
frightened her, and now the enormity of what she had
endured descended upon her and she was shaken
through and through.

Evan had gone to the fireplace and worked there for
a moment with old newspapers and kindling, and
within minutes he had a fire blazing in the drafty room.
He laid several dry logs on the andirons and sat back on
his heels, watching as they caught fire and crackled and
began to flame blue and orange. Snaps of sound and
flurries of sparks flew upward. Laurel smelled the
comforting scent of wood burning and moved near to
the fireplace.

Evan went into the small kitchen, found brandy,
glasses, crackers, and an unopened jar of peanut but-
ter. He brought them to where Laurel sat huddled in
front of the fire, poured brandy into a glass, and
handed it to her. "I apologize *most* humbly," he said

sarcastically, "that there isn't more suitable cuisine for you here in this backwoods abode." He bowed, the irony in his eyes like a barrier between them. "Drink it," he ordered. "It'll warm you."

Laurel did not like the taste of brandy nor the way it burned as it went down, but it did warm her; she sipped it slowly and let its warmth flood through her cold body. In a short time it and the fire before her dispelled the chill that had gone deep into her body, bringing a dizzy sort of drowsiness to her whirling thoughts. Lassitude crept over her senses. The fire sent its growing warmth through the cabin, giving it a snug, lulling atmosphere, pushing the storm away so that it no longer seemed so near and threatening. Now it had become only a distant, gusty roar.

"You'd better get out of those clothes," Evan advised her curtly. "They'll be wet when the snow on them melts. I'll get you a blanket to wrap up in."

He went away and returned in a moment holding a folded Indian blanket out to her, which she accepted without acknowledgment or thanks.

She sat still, sipping the brandy, gazing into the flames. Tiredness held her there, unwilling to move. This was the way she wanted it, she thought. This was the way she wanted to remember Evan Templar, if and when the memory of his dark and seductive face, his lean and powerful body, ever crossed her mind in the future. This dismal interlude would be a perfect antidote if ever she found herself remembering that she had desired him.

After a while Laurel's garments began to dampen into sodden layers of cloth, and she realized that once again Evan had been right; she would have to remove them. She picked up the blanket and stood, glancing at him. He had made himself at home, had found candles and a book, and now he sat relaxed in a chair, his nose in the pages, apparently oblivious to her presence.

She saw that there were two doors leading off the main room. One of these opened into the little kitchen, and the other into a small bedroom in which she saw a narrow bed and other furnishings that suggested occupancy by only one person. What had Evan's father been like? she wondered idly, removing her wet ski clothes. Undressed, she rubbed her stiffening muscles and wrapped the blanket around herself, and then she went back into the main room, carrying her wet things. These she draped in front of the fire to dry. Evan had already done so with his own clothing and now he, too, wore a blanket. The room glowed with the mellow warmth of the fire and the candles, and smelled pleasantly of burning wood and candle wax. She walked a bit unsteadily to the fireplace and sat down again. Evan did not stir.

The wind shrieked outside, and now and then there came a sound like thousands of bits of sand or gravel being flung at the windows. It was icy snow, windborne, flying against the glass. Inside, warmed by the fire and the brandy, Laurel sat listening to the sounds of weather she had never experienced before, her heart heavy within her. She felt her growing weariness displace the anger and hurt, and at last her mind drifted and she dozed, her body slumping against the high stone hearth.

In the night Laurel awakened to discover that she was lying down, that her blanket was gone and she was between smooth sheets—and that Evan Templar lay sleeping beside her!

Disoriented, her mind still weary and dazed, she

tried briefly to puzzle it out, found it too difficult, and let it go as sleep engulfed her again. She turned, moving closer to Evan, laid her hand on his chest, and felt the crisp, wiry curls of hair there.

The wind outside had softened into a murmur, the sleet had stopped, and she was only barely conscious of where she was—next to Evan, his arm cradling her to him on the narrow bed under the sheet and the thick woolly blankets, his body relaxed as he slept. He moved slightly, nestled her nearer to him, and turned his face toward her so that his cheek rested on hers. Without noticing, she drifted back to sleep.

It was late morning before the leaden light of an overcast day filtered into the room and awakened Laurel. She stirred, opened her eyes—and saw that Evan was awake too. He was still lying beside her, watching her intently, his eyes soft, his face boyish, his tumbled black hair a mussed dark cloud on the pillow they shared.

His arm still held her beside him. Now he drew her closer and touched her face with his free hand, smoothed her hair, touched her forehead with his warm lips. And then he was kissing her throat, her face, the little pulsing hollow of her shoulder, her mouth . . .

Sleep washed out of her like a fast-ebbing tide. Laurel tried to struggle away from him, but he held her fast. Wide awake, she felt his hard body pressing close to hers. Stirred by his kisses, her body was swept by the tempest of wanting that he always aroused in her, but the memory of his callous behavior of the night before bade her not to respond. Echoes of his words and the way he had looked, the memory of the way he had closed himself off behind a barrier of icy indifference, flashed through her mind even as desire coursed through her body. He was kissing her gently, long and softly, his breath catching and shuddering. The war that raged inside her intensified; then his relentless strength overpowered her outrage, and as the long seconds passed and he lay holding her and kissing her, her anger melted away.

There was only wild wanting, the longing that came with his kiss, rising like a wind and igniting her body's deep, secret places with a fire that could not be denied. His kisses grew harder, more demanding. His free hand touched her breasts with knowing, teasing caresses, and desire inflamed her, spreading through her whole being the way the brandy's warmth had done the night before. Afire with the wanting he had awakened within her, she answered his kiss; his kiss grew more possessive now, open, wet, his tongue touching the recesses of her mouth and tasting her lips.

Evan was above her now, holding her beneath him, searching her face with his knowing eyes. She knew that he could read her thoughts and feelings, though he said nothing. His hands caressed her breasts, stroked them, moved with practiced knowledge to bring her to even greater heights of desire. His breath was warm on her throat. She lay unmoving and silent, looking into his eyes, waiting, knowing the feel of his weight, his hard tanned body upon hers.

They lay in the winter morning's dull light and his eyes slowly traveled over her body, gazing at her almost lovingly. He said, "Laurel, you're so beautiful. . . ." He sighed, and then he was kissing her again, this time as gently as the touch of a rose petal. He bent to touch the exposed tips of her bare breasts with his open lips. He moved to hold her more closely, his dark head upon her breast, the hard muscular strength of his body pressing against her.

She closed her eyes and let the cascades of desire course through her. Like little torches, they brought an agony and a rapture she had never known existed.

Evan kissed and caressed her until she felt as though she could bear no more. Aroused to heights of wanting that consumed her, demanded fulfillment, knowing that it was no longer possible to hold back, she gave herself up to the wildly mounting passion and breathed his name softly. "Evan . . ."

"Yes, my darling. Yes."

"Please. . . ."

"Yes. . . ."

He saw in her eyes the immensity of her desire, which was reflected and intensified in his own. She knew instinctively that this moment was a special and unique one, that she was poised between all that she had known before and what now, with Evan, she would learn.

Without regret she let go of the last lingering thoughts of innocence. Let it happen, she thought. It didn't matter that he did not love her; it didn't matter that she was only the latest in a long line of conquests to him. To her, it was to be the giving of love.

Evan moved away from her briefly and she saw his body. Unashamed, she looked. It was beautiful, like the statues of Adonis at the museum, or Michelangelo's David—but living, warm, sweet. She waited. He moved his hands on her body, touching her breasts, her thighs, and her hand, as though possessed of a will of its own, reached out to touch him in return.

Abruptly, Evan sat up. He left her side and got out of the little bed, moving with feline grace. He went to

the window and paused, looking out at the drifted
snow. Puzzled, Laurel watched him. She did not understand until she, too, heard the sounds that had sum-
moned him away from her.

People were coming!

The sounds of voices calling their names came
faintly, muffled by the blanketing snow. Laurel
watched as Evan half turned toward her, his hand
extended in a gesture that meant *listen*. He uttered a
short, explosive curse, then said, "Somebody's out
there."

From outside, she heard a man's voice say, "They're
here! Well, *somebody* is; there's smoke coming out of
the chimney!"

Cameron!

Laurel sat up, covered herself with a blanket, and
pushed her hair back. She realized that of course
people had been out looking for them; there were
probably several rescue teams out combing every inch
of terrain between the ski lodge and the castle, in touch
with each other by CB radio.

Quickly Laurel dashed from the bed and ran to the
little bathroom. Evan had gone to the other room for
her clothing, dry and warm now, and he brought it to
her, handing it to her through the half-open door. As
she dressed she heard him doing the same in the
bedroom. By the time the voices came near enough for
her to identify the others with Cameron—Mr. Cain was
there, and Toddy, the Winterfire groom—Evan had
finished dressing and gone to greet them at the cabin
door. And by the time they had removed their skis and
snowshoes and stomped their feet free of snow and
come in, Laurel, fully dressed, stood smiling in the
cabin's main room.

Her *face* smiled. Inside, she was miserable. Her head
ached, her muscles were sore from the previous day's
unaccustomed exercise, and she was trembling. A knot
of chill, heavy tension had gathered within her body,
the echo of so much unsatisfied wanting. But the pain
that was even greater than these came when her eyes
met Evan's and she saw his bland, uncaring expression.
She saw how little her gift of love would have meant to
him; he was only angry that they had been interrupted,
merely disappointed, not bereft.

The expression of love that would have meant so
much to her would have been for him a mere diversion,
another triumph, just another momentary bit of enjoy-
ment.

Everything after that became a flurry and a blur in
Laurel's memory. They were bundled into their parkas
and taken back to the castle through the dim, cloudy
winter noontime and their rescue reported to all concerned parties. The story of how they had been caught
in the sudden storm and found their way to the cabin
was told and retold; all rescue personnel were thanked
and thanked again. And at last they sat in the library at
Winterfire, avoiding each other's eyes and saying nothing to each other.

Denise tapped at the door, came in, and said to
Laurel, "Excuse me, I know you're probably exhausted, but maybe it would be a good idea for you to
call Mr. Bellamy as soon as you feel up to it." She
seemed not to notice any tension between Laurel and
Evan. At the mention of Richard's name, Evan's jaw
muscles hardened. "The phone lines were fixed this
morning and he's called several times."

"Thanks, Denise; I will." Glad of the excuse to
escape Evan's presence, she left the room and went

upstairs. She closed the bedroom door and leaned against it for a moment, closing her eyes. What could she say to Richard? What was there to say? she asked herself wearily.

But if she didn't call, he would only keep phoning. Maybe he would even take it upon himself to visit.

She opened her eyes and crossed the room to the bed. Sitting on the edge of it, she lifted the phone and heard the welcome sound of the dial tone, a sound that had been missing for some time. She was about to dial when she heard a soft tap at her door. She replaced the phone with a sigh and went to open the door.

Evan stood there, his face remote. "Laurel, I came up here to apologize."

Remembering how brutal and unfair he had been the night before, she said, "It's all right. I guess I was pretty unreasonable too."

"I don't mean . . . last night. I mean this morning. I'm sorry."

Laurel understood all too well. The slow flush of humiliation flowed into her cheeks. He hadn't wanted her at all.

"Will you forgive me? It will never happen again. I don't know what came over me. I . . . I want you to know that. And to say you'll forgive me. Will you?"

She turned away from him. "There's nothing to forgive."

"Please."

"All right. You're forgiven." Her nerves were still taut, her head still ached. With more irritation than she meant to convey, she said, "Now, if you'll excuse me, I have to call—"

"Oh, yes, you have to call Mr. Wonderful! By all means, do go ahead. Right this minute, before he dies of anxiety. I shan't keep you." And with a formal little bow that said even more than his cold words had, he left the room, closing the door behind him with eloquent politeness.

It took Laurel nearly half an hour to convince Richard that she was all right, that she had suffered no permanent ill effects from her experience in the blizzard, and that there was no need for him to fly to New York. He was concerned at first about her physical well-being, and when she had assured him that she was perfectly fine, she was surprised to hear him say, "You were alone in an isolated cabin all night with a man. That's what I was told. Well?"

"Well, what?"

"Well, is it true?"

"Yes."

Impatience and exasperation mingled in Laurel's feelings. Richard's attitude was amazing. How had he come to assume this pompous, proprietary tone?

"You don't sound exactly penitent about it."

"Why should I be? We were lucky to find the cabin."

"Look, Laurel, I'm a broad-minded man, and I love you a lot. But I just can't understand how you could have allowed yourself to be placed in such a . . . a compromising situation! Surely there must have been some way you could have gotten out of there and back to the castle?"

"No, there was no way."

Silence. Then: "It's going to be a bit hard to forget that the woman I plan to marry spent a night alone in a snowbound cabin with another man."

Laurel said nothing, and felt nothing but irritation toward Richard. She wondered what it had ever been that she had felt toward him that she had mistaken for love. She held the phone away from her ear, listening to him wearily.

"So, tell me, I have to know: When are you coming home? You've already dawdled there far longer than necessary. I want you to make your reservations as soon as I hang up and get back here where you belong."

Finally she spoke. "Richard, I'll be there when I've finished my assignment. I haven't done so yet; I'll need more time."

"More time? What for?"

She sighed. "Goodbye, Richard." She replaced the phone and put her hand to her forehead, willing away the ache that throbbed dully behind her eyes. Why hadn't she said it? Why hadn't she simply told Richard, "I don't love you. I can't marry you."

But Richard was right about at least one thing, she thought. There was no logical reason for her to stay on at Winterfire. If nothing that had happened before this morning had proved that, then what almost happened at the cabin certainly should have. She was only asking for heartache, or worse, by remaining here.

She would make her reservations and leave. If the missing pages turned up before she left, fine. If they didn't, well, there wasn't a thing she could do about it. Staying on wouldn't bring them back, and they could always be shipped to the museum.

And whatever Evan was planning to do to try and get them back didn't include her; he had made that crystal clear. So there was nothing to detain her at Winterfire.

Once back in San Diego, she would tell Richard, in person, that she could not go through with marrying him. And somehow she would make Dr. Spence realize that what had happened to the papers had not in any way been her fault. She would do her best to convince him of that—and hope that he would believe her.

This trip had wrought havoc in her life. Nothing was the same, nor would anything ever be the same again. She hoped that out of the wreckage she would at least be able to salvage her job.

Chapter Seven

The airline reservations clerk told Laurel that flying across the country just now was tricky and unpredictable. So many winter storms had closed airports and rerouted flights that there was no guarantee when she could take a flight. The best he could do was to put her on standby, promising to call her as soon as the weather cleared.

She wavered about calling Dr. Spence. Her head ached and she was still tired from her ordeal. She decided to take a long, hot bath and relax, then perhaps have a nap and call her boss later.

When she awakened, it was late at night. No sound disturbed the silence of the castle, and still she felt exhausted. She slept again.

Light from the dawning sun touched her face and she came awake to bright flashes of gold. The sun's yellow rays came shimmering into the room, sparkling with

blinding brilliance on the mirror. The whole eastern sky
was molten gold and pink cloud-dappled turquoise, the
snows lit with a metallic splendor. The long hours of
sleep had healed her aching muscles, banished the
headache, and restored her spirits.

From her window she saw a scene of such beauty that
she caught her breath. Rays of fire from the rising sun
sent long purple shadows across the landscape like
beckoning fingers. Each tree was outlined in blazing
light and the world was a charmed place.

Laurel dressed quickly, putting on white woolen
slacks and a gold blouse, a warm chocolate sweater-
coat that enveloped her from chin to midthigh, a
brown-and-gold scarf and her white boots and mittens.
She rushed out and down the stairs, hurrying to beat
the sunrise before it could fade; she didn't want to miss
a second of it!

Sounds and fragrances came from the kitchen, where
Bridget was preparing breakfast. She smelled sausage
and yeast bread, aromatic coffee and cinnamon, but
even though she was beginning to be hungry she did not
pause or hesitate for a moment. She went through the
entrance hall and outside, breathed deeply of the clear
air, and felt its incredible warmth. Everything seemed
to glow, as though lit from within. She walked out and
away from the castle, reminding herself not to go too
far lest she anger its ruling monarch again—and suddenly she stopped. There was the unexpected flash and
dip of a scarlet bird flying low over a bank of unbroken
white, its glittering splash of color startling her momentarily. Then she saw that someone had sprinkled grain
generously on the smooth snow. This lone cardinal was
the first hungry arrival. Without turning, hoping not to
frighten the bird, Laurel took a few steps backward—

and bumped into someone. She gasped and turned around.

It was Evan, standing there in a sheepskin coat, its front unbuttoned to the warm sun's light, his chest partially exposed, his legs trim in dark, slim-cut denim. "Good morning, milady," he said without smiling. He, too, looked rested.

"Good morning." Laurel wanted to be aloof and chilly, wanted to turn and go away from him, but the joyous light all around her had enchanted her, lifting her mood. She said, "Oh, isn't it *beautiful?*"

And he, looking only at her, ignoring the flaming beauty of the winter dawn, said, "Yes. It is indeed."

They walked together, their boots leaving long dashes and dots in the snow. "What brings you out so early?" Evan asked.

"This wonderful morning," she replied. "I couldn't resist it. I love early mornings."

"Me too."

"Really?"

"Yes. It's my best thinking time."

Laurel did not inquire what the master of Winterfire thought *about*. She walked alongside him without saying anything. After a moment he said, "I've been thinking about getting back to work. I'm not always a do-nothing, you know."

The cardinal had been joined by other birds now, and they were raucously devouring the grain. The sounds of their screeches and flappings brought even more birds. "What sort of work do you do?" Laurel asked. It had not occurred to her before that he had an occupation, or needed to do anything. Again she realized that there were many things about him that she did not know.

He did not answer for some time. Then, suddenly, as though having debated something in his mind and reached a decision, he said, "Well, why *not* tell you? Maybe I ought to; maybe it's a stupid idea and I should talk to somebody about it, just to see what they think. Let's sit over here." He took her gloved hand, led her to a snow-covered bench, brushed it clean, and they sat down. The sunlight was on their faces, warm as May. The air was windless. The only sounds were made by the birds, and now and again the far-off drone of a car on the highway. Evan said, "I've had this idea since before I went away. Maybe it's good, maybe it isn't. I'll run it by you and you tell me what you think of it, all right?" She nodded. "Before I went away, I managed the family's interests. The Templar enterprises include a lot of far-flung things, most of them pretty dull; they practically run themselves." He gave an offhand shrug, as if to imply that he hadn't cared too much for the job of dealing with them. "I turned it all over to Mr. Cain when I left, and he's done such a fine job I plan to let him continue with it. He wants to, which is fine with me. We went over it all yesterday evening. So . . . that leaves me free to pursue my idea, if I decide to go ahead with it."

"I'm intrigued," Laurel said. "What is the idea?"

He looked at her with a curious, surprised glance before he spoke again. She would never have imagined that he could be diffident, but he seemed to lack confidence about whatever his idea was. "You'll be frank?" he asked. "You'll tell me honestly if you think it's a bum notion?"

"Yes."

Evan seemed not to know where to begin. Finally he broke a small branch off a shrub beside the bench and began to draw in the snow with it, sketching maplike lines. His face was earnest and serious, and he said, "To begin with, the Winterfire acreage goes from just this side of the village, here, that's south, to the place where my father built the cabin, that's the north boundary, up *here*. That's about three miles." He made a sweeping line in the snow to indicate the northern boundary of his land. "And from the county line in the east, over there"—he raised his head and pointed toward the risen sun and the blue hills in the distance—"to the river that's a couple of miles back the other way, west, over there." He turned and pointed to the western sky, and then made marks in the snow to indicate the eastern and western limits on his map.

Clearly this idea was important to him, Laurel thought. He meant to explain it in minute detail, step by step. He spoke haltingly, pausing often to put his thoughts into proper order. Now he made a small *X* in the center of the drawing. "Here is where we are," he told her. He made another *X* at another point and said, "And the place that I have in mind, where I'll build my . . . project—that is, *if* I do—is right there. It's about a mile from here."

Now he stopped, looking confused about how to continue. "I can't really tell you about it this way. The place I'm talking about is so special, you'd have to see it to understand what I have in mind." He ran a hand through his dark, shining hair, and then a smile lighted his face. "So why don't I show it to you? How about it, would you like to take a ride over and look at it? Then you can get a picture of what I'm talking about."

Pushing far back into her mind thoughts of calling Dr. Spence and staying within reach of a phone in case the airline called, Laurel smiled and nodded. "I'd love to see it, Evan." Hearing herself say it, she was surprised, but there was something magical about the morning, and suddenly she knew that the most appealing thing she could do on such a day was to go for a ride in the snow with Evan Templar.

"Wait right here. I'll only be a minute." Evan leaped up from the bench and headed for the garage at the north side of the castle. Within a few moments Laurel heard an engine start, and then he backed out and drove along the road toward her in a four-wheel-drive vehicle that looked as though it could handle any sort of terrain, snow-covered or otherwise. He halted near the bench. "Hop in!" he called, and she ran to the passenger side and jumped in beside him. His face was filled with something young and carefree and joyous, something that touched Laurel's heart. If only he could be this way more often, she thought; if only he could be this happy all the time!

The bright morning glowing all around them, they bounced along over snow-packed back roads, the vehicle holding to them easily. They passed vast fields of unbroken snow and thick groves of pine and hemlock, and Laurel was awed by the broad winter landscapes. Evan explained that the same long-ago glacier that had crept down from the polar ice cap and gouged out the finger lakes and made the drumlins had also created this low, rolling terrain. "Ten thousand years ago during the Ice Age these glacial deposits were left behind," he said. "They're called moraines."

Laurel saw frozen brooks and waterfalls that spilled over sheer cliffsides, wandering lichen and moss-encrusted stone walls and clumps of trees the snow had outlined with puffs and beards of white. Soon they were on a road that climbed a gentle slope up an angled plain, and at its summit Evan parked the Jeep and they got out and walked to the edge of the slope. The slope, a high meadow in summer, ended abruptly in a cliff, and the view from this vantage point was seemingly endless. Laurel caught her breath and gazed in wonder, shading her eyes with her hand.

The mountains in the far distance were pale blue against the morning sky's darker blue, their peaks outlined now with gold and silver. Magnificent splotches of snow-drenched forestland, open fields of silver snow, and gunmetal-blue rivers, slow-moving, bearing white specks that were miniature icebergs, lay on the valley floor. Evan watched Laurel and waited for her response.

When she spoke her voice was soft with rapture. "It's utterly breathtaking!"

He was pleased. He gestured with his open hand, indicating the far-below scene. "Not many people ever see this. It's far from the main road, and private property besides. In a way it's like the papers, hidden away from everybody but the few who happen to have ownership." He paused, gazing out across the vista. "I've always loved to come here. It's one of my favorite places." He laughed, and it was a shy, hesitant laugh. "But, you see, I don't think it should be just for me alone. That's how I got the idea."

"What *is* your idea, Evan?"

When he spoke again, she was aware of another new and unsuspected facet of his complex nature. There was a kind of reverence in his voice. "It's this," he said, speaking simply, apparently wanting to say it and get it over with and find out what she would say about his idea. "I thought of building a . . . a kind of winter park, I guess you'd call it. Not like the ski lodge, not like anything that's already here in the area, but a place for people to come who'd like to enjoy the surroundings. There would be outdoor activities if they wanted that, or they could swim or play tennis or do other things indoors. Or they could just sit and look out. I thought I'd have it so people could skate or toboggan or build ice sculptures or whatever, but not ski; nothing here would compete with anybody who's already in business here. The idea would be to help them, to bring more people in. I haven't decided yet whether to have it just for winter guests, or all year round. It's beautiful in summer too. What I mainly have in mind is just sharing this particular spot with other people, I guess. . . ." His voice trailed off as he gazed at the panorama that lay gleaming in the sunlight below.

When Laurel realized that he had finished what he was going to say and was waiting for her reaction, she turned, and what she saw on his face melted her heart. He was as eager as a small boy offering one of his treasures to someone very important. He was sincere; he was vulnerable. He was awaiting her verdict. With a pang she understood that this idea was terribly important to him. She said quietly, "Evan, it's one of the most exciting ideas I've ever heard!"

"You think so? Really?" His eyes gleamed.

"Yes, I do!"

And then they were both laughing and Evan had grabbed her in a hug that pushed the breath from her body and spun her around. In her mind she could almost see Evan's dream as clearly as he could.

He set her back on her feet again and grabbed her hand. "Come on!" He laughed, excitement dancing in his eyes. "Let's go down to the village. I want to talk to Mr. Cain about it right now. Why wait? You say it's a

good idea—and that's enough encouragement for me!"
They ran back to the Jeep, and Evan expertly turned it
about and drove down. "And we can have a look at the
plat books. I'll have to figure out how much new road
will have to be built to connect the ridge to the main
highway and . . ."

As they went, the idea for Evan's winter park took
on weight and substance, light and shadow, as though it
already existed. The more they talked about it, the
more it became an established fact. Another strange
thing happened, too. As they shared in planning it, the
idea subtly changed from being Evan's to being *theirs*.
By the time they reached the tiny village in which Mr.
Cain had his law office, it was as though they had
created the whole plan together and were still planning together, yet neither of them seemed aware of
the oddness of this.

Nor did Laurel remember that by now she should
have talked with Dr. Spence, and also, in all probabil-
ity, had she remained at Winterfire today, that by now
she would have heard from the airline. Richard Bellamy was even farther from her thoughts. The world
was bright, and Laurel's heart was singing; she was
alone with Evan Templar, beside him as they drove
through the sunlit winter morning, and nothing else
seemed to matter.

Mr. Cain heard Evan out without interruption, interest shining in his bright, intelligent eyes. When Evan
had finished, the lawyer ran his hand through his hair
and nodded. He asked a question or two, listened as
Evan answered, and smiled. After a few thoughtful
moments, he spoke, and what he said was enthusiasti-

cally positive. He was almost as excited about the idea as Evan and Laurel had been.

"I'm delighted with the idea," he said. "It sounds like a project that will benefit everybody in the area." Then, rising, he said, "You almost missed me; I have to leave in an hour for Albany. Let's go have a bite of lunch." It was only then that Laurel realized that she was ravenously hungry; she hadn't eaten in almost twenty-two hours.

The three of them had lunch at the village's best restaurant, an Alpine rathskeller that captured Laurel's fancy at once with its old-world charm. They ate thick steaks and salads and Black Forest cherry cake and drank mugs of hot coffee. As they ate they exchanged more thoughts about the winter-park project. Mr. Cain left shortly after lunch was over, and Evan said to Laurel, "Let's go look up the plat books. We can get at least a rough idea of how much road will be needed."

The afternoon sped by. They pored over the huge old books of yellowed survey maps, calculating miles of road and numbers of dollars and workmen and the like, and it was nearly sunset when Laurel belatedly noticed the time. The whole day had flown!

As afternoon grew into evening they gathered up their notations and left the building in which they had worked all afternoon. Laurel thought that not only the sunrise but the whole day had been magical, like a gift, something to be remembered and cherished. Evan had been so full of enthusiasm and joy; not once had he lapsed into his chilly silence; not once had the old pain crept into his blue-green eyes. The day had been beautiful in every way. But now it was ending. . . .

She sighed. Evan, holding her arm, walking beside

her toward the Jeep, turned to look down questioningly at her. "Why the long, sad sigh?" he asked.

"Oh . . . nothing."

"It was something."

"Well, it was just . . . today was so lovely. I hate to see it end."

"Well, then, let's not let it!" he said, his mood still light and filled with enthusiasm. "Come along, milady. Let's see what sort of mischief we can find to get into." And, laughing, they ran the rest of the way to the Jeep.

Dinner at the rathskeller was quite different than lunch had been. The spacious dining room that had been sunlit at noon was dimly lighted now, soft music was playing, and the table to which the waiter led them, a small corner one, had an air of intimacy. Evan's eyes glowed and he smiled across at Laurel, and she felt again the incredible warmth and pleasure that his lighthearted mood created within her. Over glasses of wine they talked about the winter park, about the day, about other things. . . .

And then, making conversation, Evan asked, "Did you speak with your boss yesterday?"

The question brought back all the dull, unwelcome things she had pushed out of her mind. "No."

"You didn't? I'd have thought you'd call him about why you've been detained."

"I was going to. But I didn't. I know I have to . . . but—well, I hate to. I know how upset he'll be about the missing pages. And if there's a chance of your actually getting them back . . . well, maybe it won't be necessary to tell him at all. I'd certainly prefer not to have to; it might be a lot of pain for nothing. Do you have any idea how long it might be before you'll have them back?"

Evan did not answer. He studied the pale wine in his glass, his face unreadable. Something had come between them, swiftly and undeniably. She asked, "Evan, you *do* still think you can get them back, don't you?"

He looked at her blandly and said, "I hope so."

"Well, have you done . . . whatever it is that you were planning? Have you tried to get them back?"

Something rippled across his face, something unpleasant. "No."

"But why? Evan, you know how important the papers are to me . . . to the museum. And *time* is important. You said—"

"I know perfectly well what I said! Please don't ask questions, Laurel. I can't tell you anything. Not yet."

Her chin came up and she gazed at him levelly. The magic had gone; now there was a gathering cloud to dim what they had shared. "You haven't even tried. . . ." She could not disguise her disappointment in him.

"Laurel," he said, and there was a certain menace in his look, "I've told you to stay out of this, not to meddle. If you must know, I haven't done anything about the missing pages because something I've been waiting for hasn't happened yet. Someone hasn't . . . done a certain thing. And there has to be the right psychological moment. That's all I can tell you. So just stop asking, all right? As I said before, *stay out of it.*"

Laurel looked across the candlelit table at him and wondered how anyone could be so wonderful, so much fun to be with, as he had been all day and then, as suddenly as a chameleon and with as little provocation,

change into the dark, brooding, secretive, closed-in
person he was now. The barriers that had been down all
day had come up again. Evan's eyes no longer glowed
with happiness; now they were guarded. She felt a
tangible chill, as though she had been in bright sunlight
and a cloud had appeared to hide it.

Laurel sipped her wine, contemplating him in baffle-
ment. The antagonism was back, the challenge. As she
tried to puzzle out what had happened, somewhere
deep in her mind a strange new suspicion began to
gnaw at her. Had Evan only been using the fact that
someone had taken the pages to prolong her stay at
Winterfire? Did he have some reason, some purpose of
his own, for wanting her to stay on? What could his
reason be?

Then she realized what that reason could be, and she
colored and looked away from him. No, it was ridicu-
lous. Or was it? Hadn't he said that she *had* to stay on
until he had decided she could go? But that had been
before the pages had been taken, and before she had
known that he had intended to give the papers to the
museum all along.

Considering the possibilities, she watched Evan sur-
reptitiously. There was no way she could read what
went on in his mind. When he withdrew behind that
impenetrable veil, when he chose to close her out,
there was no understanding him. No, she could not
trust him. And she could not be certain that he
would—or would not—do *anything*.

Then she had an even more disturbing thought. Had
he taken the pages? Had he done it himself, and hidden
them away, and then told her he would get them back
for her? Was he using the missing pages as a kind of
bait, knowing how important they were to her, know-

ing that there was almost nothing she would not do in order to get them?

She tried to put the suspicion out of her thoughts. She did not want to think him capable of such deception. But some of what he had said came back to her, and the more she thought about it, the more she had to accept the possibility that Evan himself, for his own secret reasons, had taken the missing pages.

They finished dinner in almost total silence. Evan, distant and morose, hid himself behind the mask that had again slipped into place, while Laurel's mind was busy with the unwelcome questions that had surfaced.

By the time they left the rathskeller and were on the way back to Winterfire, Laurel had come to the conclusion that Evan had either taken the pages himself, or he had no intention of finding out who had taken them. And that if the missing pages were to be found and restored to the collection, it would be up to her to find them.

Later, in her room, she made her plan. The first place she meant to look for the missing pages—of course—was Evan's room.

If he *had* taken them that was most likely where he would have put them, certain that she would never dare to look within the sacred confines of his own domain.

If he hadn't . . . well, then she would search elsewhere—the archives, tomorrow. The solarium. Maybe even the other, unused bedrooms. The missing pages had to be *somewhere*.

But she had come to the almost certain conclusion that she would not have to look any farther than Evan's room. The only problem would be to get into it without being found out.

She listened to the night sounds within the castle,

hoping that Evan would go out somewhere so that she would have time to search his bedroom. There was no sound to indicate where he was; she had heard nothing for an hour. He had gone out to the stables right after they had returned, as he always did, to spend some time with Sultan; she had gone to her room. As the silent moments went on and on it occurred to her that she hadn't heard him come back inside. Maybe he had gone somewhere directly from the stables.

Maybe he had driven off; she could not remember whether she had heard a car leave or not. But she was sure she had not heard the sound of an outside door opening and closing.

She grew more agitated and impatient as the moments ticked by. Even if he was in the castle, she thought, he could be downstairs in the den, reading, or in the library, or anywhere. If she could have just a few minutes in his room, she could surely find the pages. By now she was convinced beyond any doubt that that was where the pages were.

The clock chimed eleven. Where was he?

She opened her door and stood listening to the silence. Then, slowly, poised to dash back into her room, nerves taut, she went out into the hall. Dim lights burned along the wall. There was no movement, nothing. . . .

She moved as silently as a shadow. Approaching the door he had said was his, her heart in her throat, she held her breath. She did not let herself think of what she would say if he caught her; she moved with the stealth of a burglar, pausing after each step or two to listen for any change in the atmosphere of the castle, anything to tell her where he was. She heard nothing.

She reached his door and stood there as rigid as a

statue for a moment, waiting for her heart to stop its pounding. Not even the smallest sound came from behind his door.

She reached out her hand and it trembled as she touched the doorknob. What would she say if he was inside and she went in?

She decided to knock, to invent some excuse, make up something to say if he came to the door. She tapped softly on the door and waited. There was no response.

It was as though she had the castle all to herself. Taking a deep breath and relaxing a bit, she reached again for the doorknob.

Evan opened the door and reached out with one great powerful hand and caught her wrist and brought her inside in one fluid movement. She gasped, her heart thumping.

Both his arms went around her. He had taken off his shirt; his chest was bare and his arms were hard and tight around her, a vise of steel. He bent his dark head to kiss her lips as he closed the door with his foot.

Chapter Eight

Caught completely off guard, reeling inwardly with shock and the sudden wild thunderclap of feeling that coursed through her as Evan's mouth claimed hers, Laurel went limp against him. Her mind searched frantically for something that she could say, some way to escape, as the hard, merciless kiss went on and on. Evan's big towering body engulfed her small frame, and his arms around her were like tempered steel; her thoughts spinning, desire again flickering within her, she could only wait until the overpowering kiss ended and then try to think of some way to elude him.

It was then that a new thought, a new knowledge, came to her; it came so forcefully and so clearly that it washed the other thoughts away before it, like bits of debris before a cleansing tide. She knew—suddenly, utterly, absolutely—that she had fallen in love with Evan Templar.

That thought stunned her even more than the unexpected encounter with him had. As it filled her and surrounded her with its truth, torrents of wanting coursed through her, and she stood on tiptoe, her eager body leaning against Evan's tall, hard form, and reached up to encircle his shoulders and hold him close. His mouth crushed hers. Her lips parted and the kiss deepened. A rising crescendo of desire flamed through her senses. She forgot everything else, the missing pages, Evan's earlier coldness, as she melted against his body. She was unaware of anything but his masterful, powerful embrace, his bare chest with its crisp dark hair separated from her breasts by only a bit of fabric, the pressure of his body against her. Deep within her the wanting grew to an all-but-unbearable, sweet pain. She moved her hands from his shoulders to bury her fingers in his thick black hair and hold him closer to her.

When they drew apart, Evan held her face between his hands and looked into her eyes with an intensity of limitless yearning and said, "You came to me."

She said nothing. What was there to say?

He murmured, "I swore to myself, after yesterday morning in the cabin, that no matter how much I wanted you I would never touch you again—not that way. I'd never try to make love to you again—unless you came to me." His eyes were dark with passion, warm now, looking deep into hers. "I almost did something I'd have hated myself for; I almost took advantage of you. Sweet Laurel, so trusting, so innocent. I promised myself I'd never betray that trust. Unless you wanted to give your love to me . . ."

Trusting. Innocent. The words crashed in Laurel's mind. Guilt came then, guilt because of what he thought: that she had come to his room because she wanted him. . . .

He had no idea of her real motive! She looked down, feeling her cheeks flame. And he misunderstood that, too.

"Laurel, Laurel," he said, tender, gentle, holding her shoulders softly, looking at her with sweet wanting. "Come with me." He took her hand and led her toward his bed. She glanced at it and saw that it was enormous, a beautiful hand-carved wooden antique bed with the rose and the *T* prominently blazoned on the headboard, a canopy of red satin above, a silken quilted black comforter and black satin pillows, embroidered in gold, below. It *was* the room of a sensuous man. It *was* a lair. Those thoughts sped fleetingly through her mind as she let him lead her across the scarlet-carpeted floor.

He stood with her beside the great bed and spoke her name. She laid a finger across his lips. "Evan . . . don't. You don't understand. . . ."

"What don't I understand?" he asked, not really caring. He was not smiling; his eyes were tracing the lines of her face, her lips. "I understand that you came to me. That can only mean you want me as much as I want you. That you feel as I do."

She shook her head. "I don't know how you feel."

"Yes, you do. I want you. I think I wanted you from the first moment I saw you, down there in the library that day. You were so beautiful, the most beautiful woman who'd ever come to Winterfire. I've wanted you more every time I've come close to you. It's been almost more than I could do to keep from—"

She shut her eyes tight and shook her head again, interrupting him. "You don't *understand!*" she said.

But how could she tell him what she had really come to his room for?

"I do; I do understand. You and I . . . we're two of a kind. We both feel deeply, passionately. We both want to reach out and take what we want. We both live for the moment."

"No! No, that's not the way I feel at all, Evan!" She felt a lump beginning to form in her throat. She raised her chin, demanding self-control. She would *not* cry. Nor would she let him think that she had decided to give in to her emotions and come here to his room because she could no longer bear to go on without him.

"It's not?" he asked, smiling a little now. His expression said that he knew perfectly well how she felt, that he understood her thoroughly, and that he felt exactly as she did.

"No! I . . . I didn't come here to . . ."

"Laurel . . . don't lie."

"I'm not lying. I didn't . . ."

He was still smiling, indulgently, as though she were a child to be humored. "Oh, I see. You want me to pretend that we *love* each other. Is that it?"

She wrenched away from his hands, which had been holding her shoulders. "No." She stepped away from him, and a dark look of anger crossed his face. She stepped backward again, and then she could go no farther; the edge of the night table beside the bed stopped her. "Evan don't."

He took one long step and grabbed her. This time there was no gentleness at all in his embrace. He wrenched her against him, hard. He held her so hard she could barely breathe. He kissed her with savage fury. There was no way she could get away, nothing she could do; he was clearly the master here. She was defenseless against him.

His mouth was hard on hers, bruising, forcing her lips open, pressing, questing. A moan sounded deep in his throat. Laurel did not struggle. She tried not to respond, intending to fling herself away from him and rush out of his room at the first opportunity, run to her room and lock the door.

He drew away. Laurel saw the line of his bare tan shoulder, his dark hair, his hard-muscled arm. His eyes roved over her face, leaving fiery trails that she could actually feel. He looked from her face to her throat, to the mounds of her breasts under her low-cut blouse. He ran his fingers slowly from her cheek down to her hand, brought her hand to his lips, kissed its palm and touched it with his tongue. "You can't tell me you don't want me," he whispered.

He let go of her hand, meaning to lift her and lay her on the bed. She sprang away, standing like a frightened deer. "Laurel . . . I won't hurt you! Come to me, Laurel."

"No. *No*, Evan."

His darkened eyes questioned her.

"I didn't come to you . . . for that. I came for another reason. I won't tell you what it was. But"—she was breathing in short little gasps—"but it wasn't what you think. Please . . . let me go."

Now he was furious. His brows drew together in a frown and his eyes narrowed. The muscles of his jaw went rigid. "I don't believe you."

"I don't care what you believe!"

"You're lying. What other possible reason could you have?"

But she could not—would not—tell him. She stood there for a moment, wondering wildly whether or not she could get to the door and out before he could intercept her, wondering what he would do if she tried. "Evan, let me go."

His face was icy now. He said, "Go, then. I'm not holding you!"

She turned and went toward the door, expecting him to stop her at every step. He could have, effortlessly. She held her breath. She reached the door, her hand found the knob, she turned it and stepped out into the hall. She closed the door behind her. But there was no one else in the castle; she knew that if he really wanted to, nothing could stop him from coming into *her* room. He had a key, or he could break down the door.

She walked numbly down the hall, opened her bedroom door, and went inside. She closed the door and locked it. Tears had gathered in her eyes, and now they coursed unheeded down her cheeks, but they were tears of frustration and fury, fury at herself. How could she love such a maddening, unpredictable man?

To him, she was only a beautiful woman whom he desired. To her, the desire was part and parcel of her love for him, a love that could never be.

She paced the floor until her emotions calmed a little, then sat down on the edge of her bed. Evan had made no attempt to enter her room. She had heard nothing at all from outside her door. The quiet was ominous, eerie. What was he doing? What was he thinking?

She had at last gone to bed and was slowly drifting toward a troubled sleep when the telephone rang, and startled her awake. She switched on the lamp, reached for the phone, picked it up, and heard Evan's voice.

"Yes, I'd like that," he was saying. Laurel was puzzled. She frowned at the phone, confused. She wondered who had called; it must be midnight, or later.

Then she heard Charlotte's voice. There was no mistaking it, and the tone was teasing, possessive. "Then come along, darling. I'll be waiting. . . ."

Feeling her face warming with embarrassment and jealousy, Laurel quickly replaced the phone on its cradle. She glared at it as though it were alive. *Charlotte.* And he was going to her.

Laurel had not seen Charlotte since the day the pages had disappeared. Now she wondered where she had been, what she had been doing. And why was Evan going to her?

But of course, she thought, she knew why.

Then it dawned upon her that when he had left she would have the opportunity she had wanted to search his room for the missing pages. She waited, listening. She heard the small sound of his door closing down the hall, and then, a bit later, she heard the muffled noise of the front door as it closed behind him. After that, faintly, she heard a car start, and heard its sound diminish as Evan drove away down the long lane toward the iron gates.

Quickly she tied her robe about her and dashed down the hall to Evan's room. Approaching his door, fearless now, she heard the clock chime the half hour; it must be twelve-thirty in the morning. She reached the door, took the knob in her hand—and discovered that Evan had locked it behind him.

She stared at the door for a moment, surprised, wondering why he had left his room locked. Then, with a dull certainty, she knew; he had locked it because she had been right. He *had* taken the pages. They were in that room. He had locked his door to keep her from finding them.

There could be no other logical reason.

She returned to her room and her bed slowly, her thoughts circling in slow, unhappy spirals. Beneath them, like a dark shadow, lay the ugly knowledge that Evan was with Charlotte.

Laurel had never known jealousy before, but now it was there, and she recognized it easily. She did not welcome it; she did not want to harbor it within herself. But there it was, and there was nothing she could do about it.

Defeated, tired, her body aching with unfulfilled desire and her mind full of thoughts she did not want, she lay awake, unable to sleep, until she heard the clock chime four. It was sometime after that that she heard the downstairs door open and close again, and then, as Evan passed by her bedroom door, she heard him humming. Humming! she thought. He sounded as carefree as a little boy with a new toy.

She covered her ears and burrowed down into the silken nest of her bed, furious, longing for sleep. It did not come until almost dawn.

When she awakened, it was impossible to tell what time it was; clouds overcast the sky and the dull gray light of the new day beyond the window was leaden. She lay looking out, thinking that the day was like her mood. The sullen, pewter-colored sky seemed deserted by the sun that had shone so gloriously the day before.

She remembered all that had happened since that beautiful sunrise. It was as though it had all happened long ago, much longer ago than a day, and the memory of last night brought with it a dull, miserable ache.

Dressing in a brilliant crimson jersey dress—it might

help to counteract the grayness and cheer her up, she thought—she considered what she must do. She decided to try, if it became possible, to get into Evan's room somehow; if she was watchful, there would be a way.

And if she could find the missing pages, and get them and the rest of the Templar Papers into the special case she had brought to carry them in, she would pack them and her things and leave. Today. She would go to the airport and wait there, if necessary; she would take her chances on being able to get a flight to the coast despite the weather conditions. Yes, that was what she would do, find the missing pages and leave—without wasting any more time.

She would have to make sure of Evan's whereabouts; she would have to bide her time. Did he plan to go riding today? Would he be out, perhaps with Charlotte?

She finished with her hair and left the room. At the bottom of the stairs she looked about, saw no one, heard Bridget at her work in the kitchen, waited, then turned toward the library. The library door was closed. She thought she heard voices, so she paused and listened. Yes! She heard the muffled sound of a male voice coming from behind the library door. Evan? She approached the door. The voice had paused; she could hear nothing.

Evan, talking with Cameron? Denise? Who? she wondered. Then she reminded herself that she should not eavesdrop. But, she told herself, she wasn't, not really. She didn't want to hear whatever it was that they were saying. All she wanted was to find out where Evan was, if she could, and hope he would stay there long enough for her to get into his room.

And then he was speaking again, and what he was saying held her rooted to the spot. She was suddenly unable *not* to listen.

"I shouldn't have said those things," he said. He sounded earnest. "I know what I said. You don't need to remind me. I said I didn't love you, never had, never could. That long ago when I asked you to marry me I'd thought I loved you, but when I came to my senses in the Legion I knew it had been only my pride, not my heart, that you hurt. I apologize, but at the time I was angry. Will you forgive me?"

A pause. Then Charlotte's voice, cool, calculating: "Perhaps. If you really want me to, Evan."

"I do."

"Well," Charlotte said, hesitantly, weighing her words, "all right. Maybe. But what about your little playmate from California? What do you have to say about what's been going on with her?"

"Nothing's been going on, Charlotte."

"Oh?" Laurel heard Charlotte's goading, sarcastic voice from beyond the door and ordered herself to leave the spot immediately, but her feet refused to budge. "You two are the talk of the village, Evan! Not to mention the fact that she's staying here at Winterfire, with you, alone! What am I supposed to think? How am I supposed to overlook what's been happening?"

Laurel could imagine Evan's face; he would scowl now, his eyes becoming cold and dark with insulted dignity. He would be icy and withdrawn.

But no. Surprisingly, his voice sounded soft and placating. "I can only assure you that nothing has happened," he said.

"I find that very difficult to believe, Evan."

"You've no reason to be jealous of Laurel, Charlotte. She's a nice person, but . . ."

"But what? Not your type?" There was a pause. Then: "I'll admit, I *was* surprised. You never liked them so young and inexperienced in the old days."

"Charlotte, I didn't ask you to come here so we could discuss Laurel Martin. I asked you here . . ."

"For what? To renew your proposal of marriage?" It was like a challenge; Charlotte's voice was silky. Laurel burned with anger and humiliation.

"Would you like that, Charlotte? Would that please you? Would that convince you that you've nothing to be jealous about? Laurel Martin came here on business, for one purpose, and one purpose only. She came here to get the papers. As you may know, some of the pages are missing, and until they're found or returned, she can't leave. If she had them, she'd leave immediately. Those missing pages are all that are holding her here."

"Evan *are* you proposing to me? If so, stop babbling on about that insignificant child and those infernal papers of yours and come here to me!"

At last, Laurel's feet obeyed her mind. She ran, unseeing, shaken, aching, her mind echoing with the words she had heard Evan say, Charlotte's voice ringing in her ears. She dashed up the stairs and into her bedroom, her heart pounding.

He was going to marry Charlotte. The fact kept running through her mind, over and over, like a broken record. It became almost mechanical, like a metronome, blotting out everything else. The words were an epitaph; whatever she had had, or imagined that she had, with Evan Templar now lay buried beneath them.

Automatically, without thinking of what she was doing, she began to gather up her things. She took her suitcase from the closet and opened it. She set it on the unmade bed, slowly filling it as she gathered up her things and placed them inside.

She thought once or twice about going to Evan's room to look for the pages, but she could not do it. It was too dangerous; what if he came in? What if *Charlotte* did? No. She would take the pages that remained . . . and go. That was all she could do. And the sooner the better.

She finished packing and left the bedroom with the case she had brought to carry the papers. Leaving it in the hall, she went downstairs in search of Cameron. She found him in the kitchen, talking with Bridget. When he looked up and saw Laurel's face, an expression of alarm crossed his features, but he quickly erased it. "Can I help you with something, Miss Martin?" he asked smoothly.

"Yes, please, Cameron. I'd like to get the papers—what's left of them, I mean. I'm leaving."

Cameron's eyebrows went up in surprise, but he said nothing, merely went with her, key in hand. The library door was still closed. Laurel did not want to look in that direction, but she could not help herself. They were still in there. . . .

At the top of the stairs, Cameron picked up the case and carried it along. They went to the long corridor from which both the archives and the solarium branched. Cameron opened the archives.

When he had placed the remaining pages on the table before her, he said, "I'll ask Miss Jordan to come up and help you." When Laurel made no reply, he quietly withdrew. The pages were to be wrapped, singly, in protective tissue and carefully placed, without crowding, in the case. Laurel set about the task numbly, and even the beauty of the richly embossed, priceless old pages could not lift the dark mood that had settled on her like a cloud.

Denise came, greeted Laurel cheerfully, and immediately sensed that something was wrong. Laurel hardly said a word. She only wanted to finish preparing the remaining pages for transport and go.

Denise studied Laurel with a puzzled expression on her face, but she asked no questions. She tried once or twice to make conversation, but Laurel answered in monosyllables, so she gave up. They had almost finished wrapping the pages and placing them in the case when Laurel heard the door open, glanced up, and saw that Evan had come in.

"What's this?" he wanted to know. "Cameron said you were getting ready to leave. Why? You don't have all of the pages yet."

Laurel looked at him, hoping that her face was, for once, as noncommittal at his was at times. "I've decided there's no point in waiting," she said. Her voice was expressionless. "I want to get back."

Denise, mystified but perceptive, realized that something was going on that did not include her and quietly left the room. Evan closed the door after her and then approached Laurel. She looked down at the few remaining pages on the table and busied her hands with wrapping them. He said, "Laurel?"

"Yes?"

"Why are you doing this? I told you I'd get the missing pages back for you."

"But you didn't. And I don't think you intend to—or ever did intend to."

He said nothing for a few moments. "Why would you think that?"

She looked up at him, forcing a smile to her face. "Evan, it's no use. I'm going. Let's not talk about it anymore."

He looked at her with puzzlement, and then a chill crossed his features. He said, "Oh, I see. You've decided to go back to Mr. Wonderful after all. Is that it?"

"Something like that," she told him, looking back at the page she held.

"Then I certainly won't detain you." He spoke coldly. She knew that if she looked at him she would see his jaw tense, and there would be icy sparks in his blue-green eyes.

She didn't speak, just kept on working mechanically. *He's going to marry Charlotte,* her mind said.

"I'll instruct Cameron to drive you to the airport," Evan said.

She glanced up at him, trusting herself to maintain an expressionless gaze. "Thank you, I appreciate it. And, Evan, even though the Templar Papers are no longer complete, I want to thank you for them. Even as they are, they'll be of value to us."

He looked closely at her. "Laurel, damn it, the missing pages might turn up anytime! I have reason to think they will, in fact. Won't you wait just a little longer?"

"No." She finished wrapping the last page and placed it in the case, then stood up. Evan made a move toward her, but seeing the look on her face, he stopped. His face was full of questions. "Excuse me, please?" She closed the case and lifted it, then stepped around him, walking out of the solarium and leaving him there.

Heart racing, she forced herself to walk calmly to her room. She did not know how long she would be able to maintain the veneer of businesslike nonchalance that she had assumed. She had borrowed on her reserves of strength, forcing herself to shut him out; she would not allow that strength to desert her now.

Once inside, she leaned against the door, breathing a sigh of relief. She placed the case containing the papers beside her suitcase and went to the phone to call the airline. Yes, she was still on standby. Yes, it was still uncertain whether she could fly to San Diego without delays or rerouting.

"Well, I don't care," she told the harried young man. "I'm going anyway; I have to get back to the coast. Please put me on the first available flight . . . yes, today. I understand. If I'm delayed en route, it's just too bad. This is urgent."

When she hung up the phone she had an unconfirmed reservation on a midafternoon flight that would, weather permitting, take her nonstop from New York to San Diego. If there were no weather problems, she would be back in California late that night. It was still hours before flight time. Even so, she would ask Cameron to take her to the airport as soon as possible and wait there.

She went to the window. Down below, Toddy was exercising Sultan in the paddock near the stables. Sultan shone like black silk as he moved. The weather was gray and depressing, as chill and forbidding as Evan's eyes could be at times.

She felt the sting of tears and turned away from the

window. There was no reason to linger; there was nothing to hold her here.

She said a silent farewell to Winterfire and went to the closet where she had left her coat on its hanger.

Someone knocked at her door, an impatient knock, an imperious demand to be admitted.

Laurel straightened, steeling her spine and forcing her features into a mask of professional composure, and went to the door. She braced herself for another scene with Evan Templar.

Chapter Nine

It was not Evan who stood there; it was Charlotte. Hiding her surprise, Laurel tried to smile. "Yes?"

Charlotte's face was distinctly unfriendly, and triumph gleamed in her smoky eyes. Laurel could not help observing how beautiful the older woman was; her dark hair, obviously coiffed by a skilled hairdresser, framed her smooth, flawless face with a dark halo of soft waves, and she wore a neutral-colored wool dress of understated elegance. Its simple cut and flattering lines were as eloquent as a price tag announcing that it had cost a fortune. She probably spent hours every day on herself, Laurel thought, and then she berated herself for thinking it. What was it to her? This was the woman Evan loved and meant to marry. What she did was her own business.

"Come with me, please," Charlotte said. It sounded like an order.

"Where? What for?"

"You'll see. Come on, I don't have all day!" Without waiting, confident that Laurel would follow, she turned and started walking down the hall.

Laurel did follow. She couldn't have said why, and certainly she had no wish to do so, but she found herself trailing along in Charlotte's wake, the scent of an exotic perfume wafting back to her.

When Charlotte reached the door that opened into Evan's room, she paused. Glancing behind her to see that Laurel was there, she opened the door. Something about the way she did it seemed furtive. "In here," Charlotte said. "Hurry!"

"What's this about, Charlotte?" Laurel demanded, pausing before the open door.

"Come in and shut the door. I don't know how much time we have. He's in the conservatory. . . ." And Laurel watched, mystified, as Charlotte dashed across the room and opened the door to Evan's closet. Reaching so high up that she had to stand on tiptoe, she rummaged on the highest shelf; she moved boxes and books, a suitcase and a small airline bag, and at last drew out her hand, holding a large manila envelope. It had apparently been on the closet shelf, behind the other things.

"Here," Charlotte said, handing it impatiently to Laurel.

"What is this? Charlotte, what's going on? You're going to have to explain—"

"I don't have to explain anything to you," Charlotte said, her eyes glinting icily. "Just take this. It's the rest of the pages. *Here!*" And she actually shook the envelope, demanding that Laurel take it.

She did. Frowning, looking from Charlotte to the

envelope, she was barely aware that Charlotte was busily replacing everything on the closet shelf as it had been before.

Laurel carefully lifted the flap of the envelope and pulled out the contents. The missing pages were here! She held the brittle parchment sheets that looked too fragile to have withstood Charlotte's ungentle treatment. Quickly she examined them and saw that they were intact. Then she looked back at Charlotte. Charlotte had gone to Evan's night table, and Laurel watched as she placed a key there, half hidden behind the base of the lamp. It was the key to the archives— Evan's key that had been missing.

"I don't understand," Laurel said. "How is it that you knew where they were? Why are you giving them to me?"

Charlotte laughed shortly. "I was *told* to give them to you. In a manner of speaking."

"Evan told you to give them to me?"

"Who else?"

"Why, Charlotte?"

Charlotte was closing the closet door now, in a rush to get out of Evan's room. She looked almost furious, and at the same time triumphant. "Why do you think?" She had crossed to the door now and opened it. "Come on, let's go!"

Laurel held the envelope as carefully as if it were a living thing. She walked slowly toward the door while Charlotte's agitation mounted. When they were again in the hall, Charlotte seemed to relax.

"Charlotte, I want to thank you. These pages are very important to me."

"I know. They're important to me, too."

"Why is that?"

Charlotte laughed her short, cold laugh again. "Because now that you've got them you can leave Winterfire."

Laurel stared at the other woman. She was about to say, "But I was going to leave—without them—today." Something in Charlotte's face stopped her. She stood watching the woman Evan was going to marry while the pieces of the puzzle sorted themselves out in her mind. Slowly, understanding dawned. Evan *had* had the pages. He had taken them, meaning to keep them until he had had what he wanted; then he would have given them to her and let her go so he could marry Charlotte. She had been right in her suspicions! Evan had had the missing pages all the time, while he pretended he was going to try to get them back for her.

"Evan told you to give the pages to me," Laurel said. It was not a question.

"Yes . . . in a way. What does it matter? Why don't you just take them and go? You don't have to know all the details. Just be glad you've finally got them!"

Laurel looked closely at the other woman. She thought, for a fleeting moment, that she saw a kind of *fear* in her eyes. No, she thought, she had to be wrong. There was nothing for Charlotte to fear; it had been something else that she saw.

"I *am* glad. Whatever has happened, I'm glad to have the whole set of scrolls back together again."

They had walked almost to Laurel's door. "You'll be leaving right away?" Charlotte asked. She was obviously eager for Laurel to go.

"Yes. Today."

Relief was almost visible on her face as she turned toward the stairway. At the top of the stairs, she paused, then turned back to Laurel. "Evan and I are going to be married," she said. "I thought you'd be happy to hear the news."

Hearing the fact from Charlotte's smiling lips made it even more real than it had been before. Laurel felt a dull, sinking ache in her heart. She said, "I wish you well. Both of you." Her voice was toneless. She watched the other woman's lovely face with its icy eyes, eyes that seemed to pierce Laurel's thoughts.

"I'm sure you do," Charlotte said. The smile on her face was that of a woman who had defeated a rival and was pleased through and through at the result.

Laurel turned away from her and opened her bedroom door. Charlotte laughed again, the sound of it tinkling like wind chimes as she went down the stairs.

Laurel, holding the envelope carefully, went into her room. She was glad she hadn't called Dr. Spence; as things had turned out it *would* have been for nothing. He would have been terribly disturbed, dropped everything, and come to New York, or sent someone else immediately, and she would have been embarrassed because of her failure to handle the assignment. Perhaps even fired.

Now she could go back with the whole set of scrolls. The museum would have its priceless new acquisition. Never mind the inner agony she would suffer every time she thought of Evan Templar; she had succeeded in her assignment. But how would she go on living?

How would she build defenses against the thought of Evan, the reminders of him that would come every time she saw a red rose or a black horse? How would she make herself whole again? How would she ever get through the days and nights and years of her life without him?

The light in her room was dim. Someone—Bridget, probably, when she had made up the bed—had drawn the drapes. Crossing to open them, she thought of Evan, remembered what she had heard him say in the library. "Laurel Martin is a nice person, but you have no reason to be jealous of her."

And then Charlotte's taunting voice: "Evan and I are going to be married. I thought you'd be happy to hear the news."

Laurel caught the movement of something. . . someone . . . a shadow . . . and she stopped, her heartbeat suspended. Slowly rising from the shadows near the drapes, getting up out of the half-hidden chair that stood there, turning toward her, was Evan.

For a moment it was like the first day she had seen him when he had risen from the couch in the library, and her heart leaped—but then she saw his face, and there was no joy in his eyes. There was nothing but a cool, remote look on his craggy features that sent a pang through her.

She murmured something; the words spoke themselves, she didn't think them out first. "Evan . . . I hadn't expected to see you again. Charlotte gave me the missing pages; she said you told her to. Thank you."

He looked at her as though from a great distance, but his gaze was penetrating. "Are the pages undamaged?"

"Yes." She wondered why he needed to ask. He was the one who had had them all this time; he would have known if they had been harmed. But she said nothing. She was still holding the envelope, carrying it as though to guard it against any hazard. Now she placed it on the bed and opened the case in which the other pages, each separately wrapped in thin tissue, would go along with her on the plane as hand luggage. She placed the envelope in the case and closed the lid.

Evan had come to stand near her. Now he took her hand, the same hand he had kissed that first day, and turned it palm upward. He kissed it lightly, this time without lingering. Then he closed her fingers over the spot he had kissed and with reluctance she looked up into his eyes. "Do you have to go?" he asked softly.

"Yes. Of course I have to go!"

"No. You don't have to. You're going because you want to."

There was something unfathomable dancing in the blue-green depths of his eyes. Was it a memory? It flickered there like a tantalizing secret. He was waiting for her to say something in answer to what he had said. Conflicting emotions flashed across her mind—anger because he had deceived her and plotted to hold her there; bewilderment because he could be so wonderful at times, and then so locked away within himself, hidden—or cruel.

Desire . . .

And sadness, because of the way she felt about him, always would feel about him.

"Charlotte told me you're going to be married."

It was as though he did not hear her. His eyes were tracing the lines and features of her face. From behind him he suddenly brought out his hand, and in it was one single long-stemmed thornless rose the color of the rubies she had worn. He placed it in her hand and said, "Take it with you and keep it in memory of its source . . . and it will live, until I see you again."

Laurel's eyes stung. Her throat began to ache as she

heard the words; the old, old legend about the rose was happening again. The rose would live, but the lovers would never be reunited. She could not speak.

She held the rose in her hand and moved to pick up her things from the bed. And then she heard the sound that broke from Evan's throat, a low short groan, a sound of agony. Some inner barrier, some restraint within him, suddenly gave way under too much stress. "Damn it all, how can I let you go?" he asked, and then he had her in his arms, hard against the rough fabric of his shirt, the rose crushed between them, its petals falling like velvet tears upon the carpet. "Laurel, don't go. Don't go!" He lifted her chin with one hand, looked deep into her eyes as though searching for something, some part of himself that he had lost and could only find within her, to make himself complete. He crushed her lips with his own. Cradled in his arms, held fast and motionless in his embrace, Laurel melted against him, leaning into him, her body as close to him as possible, the rigid hardness of his form forcing her body into fluid compliance with his. He kissed her as though he would never let her go.

But at last he did, and stood holding her shoulders in a grip so hard that she winced. "Laurel, you do *not* have to go. Don't go back to that—that fellow—"

"Richard? Oh, Evan . . . I'm not going back to him! I'm not going to marry him."

"Good! What a relief! Listen, let me have Cameron take the papers to San Diego for you. Then you can stay."

Incredulous, Laurel gazed up at him. What was he saying? Stay? Stay at Winterfire? When he was about to marry someone else? What was he thinking?

He went on, excitedly, "Oh, Laurel, I went through hell thinking you were leaving. You will stay, won't you? Stay here with me?"

"Evan, no! How can you ask such a thing? I *have* to go."

"But you just said you're not going to marry Bellamy."

"Evan, I can't stay here!"

"I want you to. Stay here with me."

Every impulse, every feeling, demanded that she stay, but she could say nothing. It was insane, utterly senseless, even to want to remain.

Evan said, "I want you here with me. I'm asking you to stay here with me . . . always. Laurel, you'll be the most beautiful, the most beloved mistress . . ."

She heard him say the word and her heart went cold. Silently she left his arms and stepped away. She gazed at him, shaking her head *no*.

What kind of man *was* he? What kind of woman did he think *she* was? To think that she would stay at Winterfire as his *mistress*, live under the same roof with him and Charlotte, his wife! Aghast at the thought, she picked up her things and placed them by the door. She went to the closet and got out her coat and purse. She did not look at Evan again. He stood where she had left him, his eyes following every move she made.

"I see," he said at last. His voice was flat, toneless. "So you really are leaving. . . ."

"Yes."

She looked at him once more, burning the image of him into her mind, taking an indelible picture that would never be far from her thoughts. He stood rigid, a look of anguish on his face. His eyes were dark and stormy and his pulse beat visibly in the hollow of his throat. His hands, flexed into fists at his sides, opened and reached out for her.

She turned and left the room.

Closing the door behind her, reaching down to pick up her suitcase and the case that contained the papers, she went down the stairs as fast as she could without falling. She wanted to leave quickly, before she might weaken. She knew that if she did not, she might turn and run back to him—regardless. For she knew that she loved him enough . . . Yes, she loved him enough to do as he asked.

The only thing that stopped her was the knowledge that he did not love her. He wanted her, but it was not love. Love was what he felt for Charlotte. There was no other earthly reason why he would marry her.

Cameron hurried to take the cases from her as she descended the staircase. At the bottom of the stairs, Laurel turned, looking up at the portrait one last time.

Already numb and aching with unshed tears, her mind whirled with wild, irrelevant ideas. If I stayed, and someday I were to have his son, would he have hair like that, and would it fall on his forehead that way too? she thought.

Her thoughts were full of Evan Templar as she gazed up at the portrait. Cameron had already gone out and brought the car around. She could hear its engine purring, waiting for her.

Evan appeared above, looking down at her with the same longing she had seen on his face in her bedroom. He came down the stairs to the landing and stood there just below his portrait, never taking his eyes away from her face. For a moment she wavered; a part of her wanted so badly to run back to him that she could hardly bear it. It was as though there were nothing in

the whole world but that look on his face, entreating,
yearning. She wanted to feel his arms about her and his
lips on hers.

But then Charlotte came out of the den like a
sudden, shattering explosion, and the spell was broken.
Laurel saw her dash past, ignoring her as though she
didn't exist, and run up the stairs to Evan on the
landing. She cried out, laughing, "*There* you are!
Wherever have you been, darling? I've been looking
everywhere for you!" She claimed his arm and pressed
her beautiful body close to his side, then looked coolly
down at Laurel as though to say, "Well, what are you
waiting for?" It was as final a dismissal as if she had
spoken the words aloud. Evan almost seemed not to
notice what was happening, nor to know that Charlotte
was there beside him. He had not looked away from
Laurel. Unsmiling, he watched her until she turned
away and went out through the front door.

Laurel stepped out into the chill, wet, sunless afternoon. She scarcely felt the wind that whipped its icy
breath around her. She walked to the car in which
Cameron waited and got in.

She left Winterfire Castle and did not once look
back.

Laurel could hardly believe that it had been only a
short while since she had arrived at the small airport
after the flight from San Diego; so much had happened
that it seemed an eternity had passed since that cold
evening. After she had picked up her ticket she had
called Dr. Spence. He had assumed that her return to
the West Coast had been delayed by weather conditions, and she felt no need to correct that impression.

"I have the papers in the case; they'll be hand luggage," she told him. "I won't let them out of my sight."

"What time are you due to arrive here?"

"If there's no delay or rerouting on account of weather, I should be there—" She consulted her ticket and read him the arrival time, then added, "But of course it's possible we could be grounded. Or sent to some alternative airport. I'm told the weather is still pretty unpredictable east of the Rockies. Perhaps you'd better tell the press that they can come to the museum tomorrow."

"Yes, good idea. I'll meet your flight—with a couple of security guards."

Security guards, Laurel thought, again aware of how valuable the papers were. If Dr. Spence had known about Evan's having taken several of the pages, and how incredibly fortunate she had been ever to have gotten them back, he would be beside himself. She was glad all over again that she hadn't told him.

"I'll see you some time tonight, then—I hope," Laurel said. "Goodbye, Dr. Spence."

"Take care, Laurel. We're all anxiously awaiting your safe arrival. Not to mention the papers. . . ."

The small plane lifted effortlessly into the cold blue-gray afternoon sky and Laurel settled herself in her seat, forcing all thoughts of Evan Templar out of her mind. She was glad that the sky was an almost solid mass of clouds that obscured everything below. She did not want to look down and see the beautiful hills and valleys, lakes and cliffs and rolling snowfields.

The flight from New York was on time at takeoff. As they flew steadily westward Laurel was lulled by the drone of the giant engines. Again, nothing but billows and banks of cloud were visible below. She saw no cities, no open vistas of midwestern farmland, no rivers, nothing but the gray-whiteness of winter clouds, until they had crossed the towering, ice-crested Rockies. And then it was like flying into a world of gold. The sun was setting, its blazing rays warm and glowing, outlining the clouds in golden light.

Winter was getting farther and farther behind her with every mile. She was leaving it behind, along with Winterfire, and its dark and brooding master. And a part of her heart that would never be her own again.

Chapter Ten

When Laurel had told Evan that she expected the Templar Papers to be a popular attraction at the museum, she'd had no idea of how truly she spoke. It was just as Dr. Spence said: "One never knows what's going to catch the public's fancy. This is a sensation!" And it was. Something about the beautiful old parchment pages and the stories of ancient days that they told caught on like wildfire, and the resulting publicity was still growing after four days. The museum was filled with milling crowds. The media demanded more new information about the papers, more pictures, more interviews, daily. Dr. Spence and the directors were delighted.

Laurel's first days back in San Diego were jampacked with endless activity. She had never dreamed it would be like this. She had never been so busy before, and she was glad; she did not want to have time on her hands. Press conferences and receptions at the museum took up her hours from morning to night, and after each long day was over she sank exhausted into her bed. She fell asleep almost at once, too tired even to dream of Winterfire or Evan Templar.

Richard had appeared at the museum on her first day back, his face a study in bewilderment and outraged dignity. When at last she was able to slip away for a moment between interviews, she took him into her office, closed the door, and said, "I'd planned to call you as soon as I could, but you can see how it is out there."

"Yes." Seeing him again, standing close enough to him to reach out and touch him, Laurel wondered what it had ever been that had attracted her, what had made her think she could ever marry him. Now he was waiting for an apology; she could tell by the reproach on his face, the way he stood. It was his way of making her feel defensive and guilty. But it didn't work anymore.

She reached into the pocket of her jacket and brought out his ring, extended her hand, and said, "I can't marry you, Richard."

Richard glanced at the ring in her hand but made no move to take it. His eyebrows went up in shocked surprise. "What's this all about? What's the matter with you?" he asked. "I knew something was wrong when you hung up on me, but I figured if I just gave you a little time you'd come to your senses. But *this!* Why? What happened to you in New York?" He narrowed his eyes and glared at her suspiciously.

"Nothing. I just discovered that you and I aren't right for each other." She was speaking in a cool, businesslike voice, but she saw that Richard was not listening. He was thinking outraged thoughts about her totally uncharacteristic behavior, her new poise, her abrupt and, to him, senseless decision to give him back his ring. She could almost read them as they crossed his face.

"You discovered that all by yourself, I suppose," he said. He smiled an unpleasant smile. "Or did the fabulous Mr. Templar have a little something to do with it?"

"Richard, please take your ring. And let's not say anything more. I'd like to have things as pleasant as possible between us, no angry words, no accusations. Can't we still be friends?"

"*Friends?*" he asked, his voice rising. "But I love you! I don't want anybody else!" His voice was more angry than anguished. "Please, Laurel. Whatever I've done . . ."

Laurel put the ring in Richard's coat pocket. She said nothing more. He stared at her in puzzled incredulity, started to speak several times but didn't, and then turned toward the door. Before he opened it, he turned and looked back at her one last time, his eyes almost begging. She still stood where he had left her, watching him with compassion and patience. He left her office.

During the days that followed, she caught glimpses of him now and then at the museum. He no longer tried to persuade her to change her mind, but she knew that if she gave him a chance, he would. She managed to avoid him. When she had become engaged to Richard, she hadn't known what love was.

That thought brought back something Evan had said; she remembered how he had looked as he said it, and how angry it had made her to hear his words. "I thought I was in love once, but I wasn't. I'm older and wiser now, and I know, if not what love *is,* at least what it *isn't.*"

He had been talking about Charlotte, she realized. He had asked her to be his wife once before, long ago. And she had refused him. That was the thing that had happened to him, the thing that had hurt him so deeply that he'd gone away. And after five long years, when he returned, he found that he *had* loved her after all, and that now she did want to marry him.

She thought, with an ache in her heart, that Evan, at least, would have his happy ending. Though the thought of it burned and tormented her, she tried to be happy for him, but the task she had set herself was impossible. She simply could not.

Resolutely, she tried to bar from her mind all thoughts of Evan's wedding, of Charlotte, glowing like a dark jewel beside him, bride of the master of Winterfire, and she almost succeeded. Only now and then did the picture of the castle come into her mind unbidden, gleaming with the blaze of the sun's golden light, its windows reflecting it back like fire. She buried herself in work, willing time to pass swiftly so that the painful newness of the memories would fade, and along with it, the image of Evan.

The fact that the public's interest in the Templar Papers did not diminish but, in fact, grew delighted Laurel. Along with it there came a rising tide of fascination with everything related to heraldry, ancient scrolls, knights in armor, jousting, the Crusades, castles, and the Templar family's own romantic history. The media had struck a gold mine and every detail was a nugget. The glamor began on the West Coast and spread. Feature articles appeared in the San Diego press, the wire services picked them up, and they were printed nationwide.

Several weeks after Laurel's return to San Diego she opened her newspaper one day to see a story about the Templars, datelined Winterfire Castle. Gasping her surprise, she read the story at her desk. It was the first in a series, the paper said. The legends, the private things in the archives, things that had been kept under lock and key, looked after as carefully as if they had been priceless jewels, were being released to the world!

By whom? she wondered, appalled. Who would let the newspeople in, open the archives, let them rummage through the previously jealously guarded personal records of the Templars? No source was named, but the story laid the background for more installments. There, in print, illustrated with photographs of the portrait of "the present Sir Evan Templar," the castle, and the Templar coat-of-arms, was the story of the "blood feud" that had broken the family apart long ago. Sir Evan's self-imposed exile, the story of the twin sets of scrolls, and numerous other details were now fully revealed to the world.

Laurel threw the newspaper aside and went to her window. Gazing out at the stately palm trees that lined the museum's broad drive, she remembered the red-carpeted corridor that led to Winterfire's archives and the solarium. Who had led the way, who had invited the reporters in? Evan? It was unbelievable. Certainly not Evan; Evan was much too private a person. He wouldn't mind the publicity about the papers, far away on the West Coast, but he would never allow his privacy to be invaded in this way.

Had Denise done it? No. Denise wouldn't let anybody past the entrance, nor would Cameron, or Bridget.

Charlotte. Of course, it had to have been Charlotte. Which meant that Evan had had to approve.

Laurel could picture the scene as it must have occurred. Charlotte, sitting regally in one of the antique chairs that looked like thrones in the formal downstairs reception room, beaming at the newspeople. Evan at her side, his dark head bent lovingly toward her, his voice courteous as he answered the reporters' questions. And then they had both gone up to the archives, leading the way . . .

No! Laurel could not believe that Evan would change so much, no matter how much he loved Charlotte.

She picked up the newspaper and started toward her office door, meaning to show the article to Dr. Spence and ask his opinion of its source, but at that moment he tapped on her door. "Laurel," he said, preoccupied with something, his glasses down on the end of his nose, "can you help with the champagne showing for the Historical Society tonight? I know we've asked a lot of extra work of you lately. . . ."

"Dr. Spence, have you seen this?" she asked, opening the paper and pointing.

He blinked, focused his eyes on the page, and nodded. "Yes, I saw it earlier. What about it?"

"Well, I just wondered. You've known the Templars for years; do you think Evan Templar would release a story like this?"

"I never knew *him.* I only knew his father, and his aunt."

"Oh. . . ."

"But I can tell you who gave that story out. It was

Mr. Templar's fiancée. I had occasion to phone the castle a little while ago"—Laurel's heart turned over—"to request that the legal documents regarding our ownership of the papers be finalized and sent as soon as possible, for insurance purposes, and Cameron was all upset."

"Cameron?"

"Yes, it seems he and his wife and the young lady who was Miss Dana's secretary are all alone at the castle. Seems Evan's gone off."

"Gone off? When? Where's he gone?"

"They don't know where, but he left the same day you did, Cameron said. According to Cameron, the woman he's going to marry had the place full of reporters yesterday. Drove him wild, he said, and then she up and left too. That's all I know. Why?"

"I . . . just wondered."

"Can you be here this evening? I'm sorry to have to ask again, but . . ."

"I'll be here; it's all right." Laurel's mind was thousands of miles away, her thoughts whirling. Where had Evan gone? And Charlotte? Had they eloped?

Of course they had. . . .

That would probably be the final story in the series from Winterfire. "The present Sir Evan Templar has returned to Winterfire Castle with his radiant bride after a honeymoon in . . ." Laurel's eyes burned with unshed tears as she thought of it.

Laurel looked the image of professional confidence as the reception went on and on, though her mind was numb from what she had learned that day. When it was finally over, her face ached from hours of mechanical smiling and she could not have given the name of a single person who had been present, much less remember what she had chatted about with the guests. When she reached her apartment she was weary and her heart was heavy. She fell asleep the moment her head touched the pillow.

The sun was high when she awakened. Exasperated, she saw that she had forgotten to set her alarm clock. But her long sleep had rested her. She was refreshed, her eyes bright, as she quickly made coffee, started her bath running, and dialed the museum.

"I'll be a little late this morning, Maria. Tell Dr. Spence, will you?"

The switchboard receptionist said she would, and then, "There's somebody waiting to see you."

"Who? I don't think I had any appointments."

"I didn't get his name. I'm sorry."

"It's all right. He's probably from the television station. Tell him I'll be there as soon as I can."

She hurried through her bath, trying to recall whether she had told the young talk-show host to come this morning or this afternoon. She was sure she had said afternoon, and sipped coffee as she riffled through the clothing that hung in her closet. She took a thin knit celery-colored sweater from its hanger and chose a trim moss-green skirt, then picked a gold scarf from a drawer.

She brushed her hair into a loose fall of red-gold waves; there was no time to do anything complicated with it. She slipped her feet into high-heeled green suede slippers, finished her coffee, and left the apartment.

Traffic was slow, the lights were against her, and she arrived at the museum agitated and rushed. She hur-

ried up the flagstone walk, her heels tapping busily, and
went into the spacious foyer.

"Where is he?" she asked the young woman at the
switchboard.

"In your office."

"Thanks." Pausing to take a deep breath and relax
before another hectic day began, she opened the door
and went inside.

The man who had been waiting for her sat in a chair
near the windows. Light from the bright morning sun
glared around him, beaming in through the windows,
obscuring Laurel's vision; all she saw was an outline of
someone seated there, the blaze washing out his features.

Then her face went white. She gasped and stood still.
The man in the chair was Evan!

This time he did not rise lazily. He leaped up,
covered the distance between them with the fluid grace
of a great cat, and all that she saw before he gathered
her hungrily in his arms was his weary, beloved face.
He whispered her name huskily, brought his mouth
down hard on hers, crushed her in his mighty embrace,
and held her to him as though she meant life itself to
him.

When he released her after the long, long kiss and
stood gazing down into her eyes, he saw her surprise,
her disbelief, her dozens of questions, in her eyes, and
felt her touch his face as though to make certain that he
was real. His eyes devoured her. "Just let me look at
you," he said. "I'll tell you everything in a little while.
Right now all I want to do is hold you . . . look at
you. . . ."

She gazed up at him as though in a dream. Why did
he look so tired? He looked as though he hadn't slept in

days. Her heart reached out to him; her fingertips touched the lock of his hair that had fallen forward. "Evan . . ." she breathed.

Then, shaking herself out of her stunned surprise, she pulled away. "Evan, how can you be *here?*" She gazed at him steadily while unanswered questions and dizzying emotions raced through her mind. "I thought you were halfway across the world . . . honeymooning."

"*Honeymooning?* Why did you think *that?*"

"Because Dr. Spence spoke with Cameron yesterday and he said you'd gone away—and Charlotte had too. So I thought . . ."

Evan shook his head, astonished and impatient. "Everybody's been jumping to conclusions."

"What do you mean? Evan, what *is* going on?"

"Why did you think I was marrying Charlotte?"

"She told me so! And before that, I heard what you were saying to her in the library that day. I didn't mean to listen, but I—I did. I'm sorry. But I heard you proposing to her, Evan."

Evan grinned. "I wish I had a recording of just exactly what I did say in there," he said. "You and Charlotte both seemed to think it was a proposal. But it wasn't. Don't you see? I was certain she'd taken the pages, but I knew that if I accused her of it, if I confronted her outright, she'd deny it, and maybe even destroy them. Instead, I took her own ploy and turned it around. She wanted to use the pages as a weapon, or something to trade. What she wanted was to be married to me . . . oh, not that she *loves* me, nothing like that! But because of Winterfire and the other family properties and all of that. I had five long years to think about that lady, and I figured her out pretty well. When she turned me down before, she thought she could do a lot better in the husband sweepstakes, but while I was away she changed her mind and decided I'd do after all. But by the time I got back I'd learned to read her like a book. So I wasn't surprised when she removed some of the pages from the collection. She really had two reasons: to make you look bad, maybe get you fired from your job. And to use them, to trade them for something she wanted—the Templar name. All I did was let her think she had succeeded. She gave you the pages back so you'd leave, just as I thought she would. Where had she hidden them, by the way? Do you know?"

Laurel's cheeks flushed as she remembered how certain she had been that Evan himself had taken the pages—and of his probable motive. "In your bedroom. On a shelf in your closet."

"In *my* room? I can't believe it! They were there all the time we were wondering where they were."

"Oh, Evan, I thought you'd taken them!" Laurel told him. "I'm sorry. . . ."

He smiled at her, took both her hands, brought them to his lips, and kissed them both. "It's understandable. But in the future . . . please, will you ask a few questions before you go rushing around imagining all kinds of things?" His eyes were soft and loving as he gazed down at her. "That is, if there is a future for us. . . ."

"A . . . future?"

"Yes. I came here to ask you to return to Winterfire with me. To be my wife. Will you marry me, Laurel?" Now his look was uncertain, pleading, hungry. "I need you so. . . . I love you so much. . . ."

Laurel's heartbeat quickened and her lips parted. "Oh, Evan, yes . . . *yes!*" She touched his face, ca-

ressed it with her fingertips. "My love. . . ." Then, out
of the corner of her eye, she noticed for the first time
that a strange twine-wrapped bundle rested on her
desk. It was large and flattish, covered with plain brown
paper, and it had not been there the evening before.

He said, "I've been back to France since I saw you."
He nodded toward the package. "The day you left, I
booked a flight to Marseille."

Laurel's eyes widened. Marseille?

"I went to do something I told you I wished I could
do." He smiled, lifted her chin with his hand, and
kissed her lightly. He reached over and picked up the
package and placed it in her hands. It was not heavy,
but she felt that whatever was in it was very important;
certainly it had been important enough to Evan.

"What is it?"

"Do you remember I said I wished there was something I could do for the old duke? The old castle had
gone to ruin, there in France, near where I was
stationed. Well, when you told me how much the
papers that Aunt Dana gave the museum meant, I got
an idea. I . . . well, I went and acquired the other set.
The twin set to the one you've already got here."

"You bought the other set of papers? Evan, this is a
treasure! I can't believe it!"

"Take a look! They're all there."

She gazed at Evan, cradling the package in her arms.
"Oh, Evan, this must have cost you a fortune!"

"That, my love," he said, laughing, "is a matter I
shall discuss only with the IRS. Let's just say that the
duke will be able to fix up the castle now so that it's
livable again."

"So that's where you went. . . ."

"Yes."

"But . . . I don't understand. Charlotte was still at Winterfire, until the day before yesterday. She let the media people in."

"I know. When I left I didn't think twice about her being there; I just assumed she'd leave. It wasn't until I'd finished my business in France and was waiting for my flight home that I picked up a newspaper and read the story she'd given out. Needless to say, I saw red. I placed a transatlantic call—I'm not going to quote what I said; I don't even remember, I was so mad. But I called Cameron again this morning when I got to San Diego International and he told me she'd gone. I don't think we'll be hearing from her anymore."

Laurel, dizzy with all that was happening, listened as Evan explained, and for the first time in weeks she began to feel at peace. She placed the package on her desk again, looking at it with incredulous eyes. "Evan, this—together with the papers that we already have—is absolutely unique. No museum anywhere has anything like it! Dr. Spence will be simply beside himself!" She reached for the phone on her desk, picked it up, and placed her call. Before Dr. Spence answered, she said to Evan, "*He* should be the one to open the package. He will be the first person outside of your family to see these. It will be his finest moment!"

Dr. Spence picked up his phone, and Laurel could hardly keep the excitement out of her voice as she asked him to step into her office.

When he tapped at her door and then opened it a few moments later, he was treated to an unprecedented sight. His assistant, the cool and efficient Miss Laurel Martin, was kissing a tall, dark-haired gentleman, holding him as though she had no intention of ever letting him go. On her usually neat and tidy desk was a disreputable-looking package wrapped in what looked like butcher's paper and tied with ordinary string.

"Dr. Spence," she said, releasing herself from the tall man's arms, "I'd like you to meet Miss Dana Templar's nephew, Evan Templar VI, who has been all the way to France to bring something very special back to the museum. And . . . Dr. Spence, I resign. I'm going home to Winterfire."

Everything happened so quickly that afterward Laurel looked back as though at a speeded-up film of whirling colors and movement, words, decisions. She could not remember at what point each separate thing had happened, but somehow things got done, arrangements were made, and time sped by. And together Laurel and Evan, beaming, love shining in their eyes, dashed to San Diego International Airport at dusk, and a bit later they watched the lights of the city recede as the plane left the runway, eastward bound.

Later Laurel remembered bits of conversations. Somewhere far above the lonely western desert, snuggled close beside him, she said, "There are heraldic symbols for nine sons. Let's have a pretend coat of arms made for each one of ours . . . and for our daughters, too."

And later, as the plane swept onward through the night, Laurel remembered the final moments with Evan just before she had left Winterfire. "Evan, you asked me to be your mistress. You said *mistress.*"

Beyond his profile, Laurel could see the steadily winking red light beyond the plane's window, at the end of the wing. He turned toward her, smiling. "I still say it." Her eyes widened. "I said you would be 'the most beautiful, the most beloved mistress Winterfire has ever had.' Or that's what I would have said if you hadn't turned away from me that day. Mistress of Winterfire. Wife of the guy who lives there. And that's what you will be, my love. . . ."

After the plane had once again flown into the winter world Laurel had come to love, Evan asked, "When do you want to go to Paris, Athens, and Baghdad? Right away? Or later?"

Laurel laughed joyously at him. "You really don't ever forget anything *important,* do you? I don't want to go anywhere but Winterfire. With you."

"But we will. We'll go everywhere. When we can get away from Laurel Park."

"Laurel Park?"

"That's the name I've decided on for the winter park project. It's the only thing about it that I'm going to insist on—and on that I'm going to be adamant. Everything else is subject to your approval, but not that. It's Laurel Park, and Laurel Park it stays."

She nestled nearer to him as the plane droned on through the night. Cities below were twinkling pin-points of lights, like jewels tossed carelessly on black velvet. The sky outside the plane was clear, the moon almost full. Laurel sighed contentedly, her thoughts racing ahead to Winterfire.

It was the next day, at sunset, when they arrived. The long rays of the sun struck the castle's windows, trembling on the crystal glass like ruby fire. The castle itself and its great front entrance glittered like the golden doors in a fairy tale; the sun turned everything to a burnished, gleaming red-gold, like molten metal. When they had gone inside, the sunset's ruby light filled the great hall, outlining everything with a halo of rosy light. Evan said, "You see now why the castle is called Winterfire, don't you, darling?"

"I'd imagined this was why."

"But now it'll have a whole new meaning. It'll mean you, Laurel." He drew her to him, held her gently, and spoke earnestly. "You will be my winter fire. And my spring sunlight . . . my summer wine . . . my autumn warmth. You will be all of these things and much, much more to me. And I'll try to be all of them to you, too . . . for always."

"For always, Evan."

The sunset's last long rays struck the portrait on the landing, lingering on the painted likeness of the master of Winterfire. Light flashed from the great frame and its heavy chains and sparkled on the carved and gilded balustrade of the great staircase. Then as the sun sank beneath the horizon it was gone, and the entrance hall shone with the soft lights Cameron had turned on.

Then Cameron, Bridget, and Denise burst upon the scene, and Laurel and Evan knew that they had come home. Winterfire Castle was filled with joy and laughter, plans, questions, explanations. There hadn't been a wedding at Winterfire in many, many years, and everything had to be just perfect.

Laurel had chosen not to wear an engagement ring at all, only a plain gold band. This she selected in New York, along with her wedding gown. From the blaze of jewels that winked and sparkled up from their velvet lined cases she chose the rubies.

Laurel descended the curving staircase wearing an ivory lace dress that trailed its yards and yards of hand-wrought lace train richly behind her, and she carried a bouquet of Templar roses cradled in the crook

of her arm. They matched the red of the glowing
rubies. The ceremony took place in front of the fireplace in the library where she had first seen Evan, but
now the sofa had been removed and banks of ruby
roses and white baby's breath and green ferns decked
the mantel and hearth. Long lances of evening light lay
across the room as the simple words were spoken.
There were few guests, only Bridget and Cameron,
Denise and her boyfriend, Mr. Cain, Mr. Andrews
from the ski lodge, the neighbor who made the wine
cheese, Dr. Spence, and a few others.

Laurel and Evan gazed into each other's eyes, speaking the words that bound them to each other softly, in
low, intimate tones. Evan slipped the ring on Laurel's
finger, kissed it, then turned her hand and kissed its
palm, and as he did so, he read in her eyes the promise:
*This band of gold will stay where you have placed it this
day . . . forever.*

When the ceremony was over, Evan parted Laurel's
veil and smoothed it back, and kissed her long and
tenderly.

And then it was over. Denise caught the bride's
bouquet, which Laurel threw from halfway up the
staircase, where she stood beside Evan. Carrying his
bride in his arms, he continued up the stairs and down
the hall past the door that had been hers, and on to his
room. He put her gently down on the ancestral bed
where he had himself been conceived, and his father,
and every other Templar child all the way back to Sir
Evan's son and there was no need for further words
between them.

As the evening's shadows grew longer and night
gathered about Winterfire, the magnificent stag Laurel
and Evan had seen once before moved silently out of

the grove and stood in the sunset's afterglow, light catching his antlers as he majestically surveyed his domain. In the stables, Sultan nickered contentedly.

The first impatient crocuses and edelweiss poked experimental spears of life up through the blanketing snow as though to be the first in all of nature to herald the approach of spring and its lush new life.

And inside the castle, Evan gazed at his bride with longing in his eyes, and love, and the kindling fire of passion that would leap into flame and blend with hers and make them one when at last he touched her waiting body.

He leaned down slowly, and the waiting was over.

Silhouette Romance

IT'S YOUR OWN SPECIAL TIME

Contemporary romances for today's women.
Each month, six very special love stories will be yours
from SILHOUETTE. Look for them wherever books are sold
or order now from the coupon below.

$1.50 each

Silhouette **Romance**

15-Day Free Trial Offer
6 Silhouette Romances

6 Silhouette Romances, free for 15 days! We'll send you 6 new Silhouette Romances to keep for 15 days, absolutely free! If you decide not to keep them, send them back to us. You pay nothing.

Free Home Delivery. But if you enjoy them as much as we think you will, keep them by paying the invoice enclosed with your free trial shipment. We'll pay all shipping and handling charges. You get the convenience of Home Delivery and we pay the postage and handling charge each month.

Don't miss a copy. The Silhouette Book Club is the way to make sure you'll be able to receive every new romance we publish before they're sold out. There is no minimum number of books to buy and you can cancel at any time.

This offer expires May 31, 1982